CW01501854

ABOUT SELKIE SEA

The sea stole their souls. Now they want my heart.

It's 1997 and Ireland is changing, but not fast enough for me. I'm tired of this tiny village and my life of onlys. The only gay man who's out. The only son who never knew his father.

The ocean has always been my one refuge, that is, until the dawn I'm snatched up by selkies. Three men who died at sea long ago and became shape-shifting seals, straight out of the pages of an Irish fairytale. They thought they were saving me from the same fate— instead, they've bound me to them.

They can't leave my side for seven days, while I try to discover if one of them is my soul mate. A week to decide if I want to be with Cathal, whose laugh lifts the sky, or Oliver, with his charming manners and thoughtful frowns. Or bossy silver fox David, who only seems to have the frowns. Especially when he's talking to me. I'm supposed to choose only one of them or walk away from all of them.

But I'm tired of my life of onlys.

10/1/26
15/1/26

SELKIE SEA

AN MMMM FANTASY TALE

DAVIS LAVENDER

Copyright © 2020, 2022 by Davis Lavender

All rights reserved.

No part of this book may be reproduced in any form or by any electronic or mechanical means, including information storage and retrieval systems, without written permission from the author, except for the use of brief quotations in a book review.

Author logo - Qamber Designs and Media qamberdesignsandmedia.com

A Note on Selkie Sea

Selkie Sea is a medium-burn gay fantasy romance with multiple love interests (MMMM) and a happily-ever-after ending. This story is set in Ireland and written with the spelling, grammar and terminology used there.

The cure for anything is salt water: sweat, tears, or the sea.

— ISAK DINESEN

If you've ever cried in the sea,
or even in the shower,
this is for you.

CONTENTS

1997

SEVEN DAYS

"Don't you dare fall apart. Don't. You. Dare." I ease the words out between clenched teeth. Get a grip, Marin. Think of something else. Anything else.

The gusts coming off the ocean tug at my jacket and send my untucked shirt billowing. When I first put it on twelve hours ago, my black shimmer of a suit had given me shiny new hopes to match. Now my trouser cuffs are dark with briny water, freezing foam lapping my toes as I concentrate hard on the light creeping across the waves. Behind me, the sun is rising on another day in Seafort. Another day of being a social pariah in one of the most scenic places in Ireland. Emotional torment, but with a view. Some of us are born lucky, I guess.

In the clear grey dawn, I can make out a jagged triangle of rock, an island, on the very edge of the horizon. Once it was home to a colony of monks. Their bones had crumbled a long time ago, their huts tumbling into the sea. Otherwise, I'd be first in line to join them. I can't think of anything better than a place with nothing to disturb me except furious gales and the squawks of adorable puffins. When I was a kid, I'd even wished on a shooting star that I'd wake up there, safe in the stone circles of those ruins.

My mom taught me to believe in a little magic, and I used to take that a bit too literally. I made all sorts of wishes, all the time. Please let me be somewhere else. Anywhere else. I wasn't particular, and I was open to time travel, but none of my wishes had come true. Batman had never arrived to recruit me as his next Robin, and the back of my wardrobe stubbornly refused to let me into Narnia. I learned a long time ago not to believe in anything but myself. And even that belief is a little shaky right now.

I have to soothe my spinning hamster wheel of a mind. Or at least try. Take a deep breath and count backwards from 10...9...8...7....

But the mental arithmetic can't distract me from my throbbing mess of a face, complete with a bruised cheek and rapidly swelling right eye. Then there's the hollow feeling under my shirt pocket like my heart is being gouged out with a rusty spoon. At least, for a whole ten seconds, it drowns out the mocking voices echoing in my head and the jeering faces that loom every time I close my one remaining good eye.

I wade further in. The rocks under my feet are treacherous and slippery, but I've navigated them so many times before that they barely slow me down. As I move, something tugs at the bottom of my jacket, yanking me backwards. Spooked, I look over my shoulder, wondering if I'm being followed, but there's nobody there. I feel cautiously under the surface, trying not to freak out a little at the thought of coming into contact with a cold, dead, slightly disintegrating hand. That's another thing believing in magic gives you. An overactive imagination. At twenty, you think I'd have learnt how to rein it in.

A piece of driftwood jammed into the rocks has hooked itself on an inside seam of my jacket, trapping me. Grasping the material, I try to shake it loose, the grazes on my knuckles buzzing with pain. After a few minutes of pointless struggle, I shrug my shoulders, sending my jacket sliding down my arms and into the water. I stumble forward as the branch releases me. I leave the puddle of cloth where it is, half-submerged, feeling slightly guilty because I can't really afford to lose it. But then, it's not as if I'm planning on wearing it again. I don't think I'll be accepting any more invitations for evenings of public humiliation, dress code formal.

I'm not sure why I let them get close enough to find a way under my skin last night. I've learned from bitter experience to avoid those guys. Actually, that's giving them too much in the way of credit. And testicles. Those *boys*. Spoilt little boys straight out of a stereotype whose families own half the town and run all of it. I'm used to being one of their targets, considering my mom and I don't run so much as a hot dog stand.

I should have realised there was no way those idiots were going to miss the thrill of humiliating me, not after I handed them the opportunity like some golden statuette at the Arsehole Awards. Until now, my strategy has always been to ignore them, to never catch their eye. And in their case, I didn't have to pretend not to be interested in any of them. Especially not Kevin. Underneath the swagger, he has about as much personality as a boiled potato without butter. And I should know. I'm Irish, for fuck's sake. I've eaten more than my fair share.

Stretching my arms out, I embrace the waves, letting them darken the ends of my curly chestnut hair, as the shock of icy cold on my neck pulls me out of my misery. I welcome the shivers that come with it. Although I'm wary of a lot of things, other guys from my village being top of the list, I never have to be cautious in this ocean. Even with its dangerous currents. In many ways, the waters of this bay are more like home to me than the damp decrepit flat I grew up in.

"I guess I've ruined this suit now, may as well finish the job," I tell a passing seagull. It doesn't argue, and lifting my feet off the bottom I plunge face-first into the swell, ignoring the sting of salt ravaging my battered face.

I focus on my strokes as I swim out into the open sea. At this time of year and without a wetsuit, I have about ten minutes before my circulation starts to go and I lose feeling in my arms and legs. I don't intend on being out that long. Dunking myself in freezing water is a brutal and effective way of snapping me out of my self-pity.

The trouble is, it doesn't seem to be working this time. Once my muscle memory takes over, keeping my arms in a smooth rhythm, my brain has too much time on its hands.

Last night, when Kevin and his friends approached me with cautious but friendly smiles, I have to admit I was mildly curious, if a bit surprised. Were we seriously going to act like none of that other shit had ever happened? But the dance was for charity, and I was feeling charitable. More importantly, I'd been back for two weeks and I hadn't found a job yet. The tourist season was over, and things were shutting down. They had the connections I didn't, and if I wanted to do something about my perilous financial state, playing nice was a necessary evil.

Anyway, I'd been away in Germany on a swimming scholarship since we left school, and I wasn't the same person who ran off two years ago. Maybe this wasn't the same place I ran from, either. This might finally be our chance to bond over an unlikely shared passion for something quirky, like Italian opera.

I think watching too many rom coms to keep my mom company has permanently warped my version of reality. And I really should have known better. In real life, if he looks like a jerk, talks like a jerk, and acts like a jerk, he isn't complicated and misunderstood with a tragic back story and a secret passion for Verdi. He's a jerk.

My mind keeps winding back to the moment they lured me in with their friendly banter and harmless conversation. Kevin talked about working with his father and after a few minutes I was already tuning out because my boredom levels were critical. This was the guy I'd been avoiding for so long? The taunts he used to throw at me were nothing but a faint echo. Now it seemed like the worst damage he could inflict on me was send me to sleep.

I was silently composing my excuses for hitting the road when he paused his monologue, looking me up and down. "I'm nipping out for a smoke. Coming?"

When he turned and started weaving his way through the crowd, for some reason I followed, even though I never usually smoke or drink because of my training. I made a deal with myself—one puff and I'd be able to bow out politely without offending anyone. After a successful night of bridge building, fence mending and hopefully, job offers in the bag. Tick, tick, tick.

And maybe, just maybe, even though I didn't care and didn't even want it, some little piece of me needed to know what it felt like. To fit in. To be on the plus side of the equation. Probably the same illogical impulse that makes someone want to be friends with their bullies. Or even become one of them.

Sometimes I'm so fucking naïve, I even surprise myself.

The crunch of several feet on gravel as soon as we stepped into the car park was a warning siren, but by then it was too late. A tight noose of savage spite surrounded me as they circled, their faces as twisted and ugly as their thoughts.

The music from inside stopped and as I steadied myself, swearing under my breath, Kevin's words echoed against the tall concrete walls edging the car park. The ones that hid us from passers-by. And unfortunately for me, from potential rescuers.

"Do you not remember the last thing I said to you, O'Connell?"

"I remember."

"I told you not to come back."

"I *know*."

"But you came back."

"No getting anything past you, Kev," I said, and then quietly kicked myself. I would pay for that one.

"You think you're so fucking smart? So much better than me? If you were smart, you wouldn't be here. No one likes you. No one wants you here. Wanna know why?"

I definitely didn't, but I had a feeling he was going to tell me anyway. And it was an interesting question. The thing was, he had so many sticks to choose from when it came to beating me.

Stick one, no one knew who my father was. Not even me, and probably, not even him. My mom had always refused to tell anyone who she was seeing all those years ago. And it should have been nobody else's business, but if you believe that then you didn't grow up in a place like Seafort in the seventies. She might have thought she was sparing me by staying quiet. But that was a serious miscalculation that didn't factor in my generation's knack for casual torture.

Stick two, we're not exactly well off. Partly because of stick number one. As far as local gossip went, if you gave my mom a job you may as well have been putting your hand up and saying, My son's the father. Or even, I'm the father. People were grimly determined to protect their reputations. And their bank balances. That was before feisty old Mrs Casey stepped in and gave her a job pulling pints in Casey's Bar. I could never understand why my mom didn't just up and leave this place, and I'm still waiting for an answer from her that makes sense.

Stick three, I'm gay. And up until a few years ago, acting on my feelings would have been illegal. Now it makes certain people uncomfortable. And for some reason, I'm the one who has to pay for their discomfort. In Berlin, I got so used to being free, to being myself, that I came out as soon as I came back here, thinking it wouldn't be any different. I guess I didn't think that one through. It made me feel like a time traveller being flung into the past. Or someone from another planet.

I kept my expression impassive as Kevin, spit flying, went on a long and colourful rant about why I should have stayed in Germany. He was thorough. I had to give him that. And it must have been the closest we'd ever come to being on the same page. Because I wished like hell I'd stayed there too.

As the circle tightened around me, I had a hunch this was one of those times Kevin wouldn't be satisfied pounding me with insults.

And as he and his friends closed in, I realised I was spot on about them being different. Except it wasn't in a good way. Inside they were still those cruel little boys, emotionally stunted and immature. But on the outside, they were arrogant adults, with fully developed bodies and a dangerous sense of their own power. It was going to be bad this time.

Of course, I'd changed too, my former scrawniness swamped by broad shoulders and powerful legs from swimming full-time. It didn't matter. There was one of me and six of them. So my muscles were bigger than theirs—I was still hopelessly outnumbered. I'd never been one for fighting. But this time there was a distinct lack of alternative options, and I had no choice other than to fight back.

All I have to show for it now is a dull throb of discomfort and the bite of tender scraped skin. Then again, it could have been worse. I guess that was something else to be grateful to Mrs Casey for, coming across our brawl on the way to her car and rushing in to stop it, handbag swinging. My sore head only wishes she was more careful about where she aimed it.

I stop for a break, gulping in the frigid air, and as I glance towards the horizon, something draws my attention. Puzzled, I squint at it. There's another island farther out, barely visible on the horizon. Treading water, I close my eyes and slowly open them again. Still there. Which is impossible, because I know there *is* no second island, not on any map.

Intriguing as it is, there's no way of satisfying my curiosity. The distance is deceiving. My monks' refuge is on the other side of the bay, much farther than I can swim, and this island is a fair way beyond it. There's nothing to do but wonder as I turn towards the shore.

This far out, I can't see the village. Only jagged rocks and hills as old as time. It's so peaceful without other people in it. I'm against old testament style vengeance as much as the next guy, but a biblical flood might be just what the place needs. With every minute, the dread blooms inside me at the thought of going back.

I don't want to see any of them ever again. But I have to. I came back to help my mom out, and savage beating or no savage beating, I still need to find a job. That should be fun. For a second, despair takes me over, almost eclipsing the physical pain from my aching body, and a few frustrated tears leak out into the water. I hardly feel them. I can hardly feel my legs either. It's time to head home. The last thing I want to do is accidentally drown. I won't give them the satisfaction.

Just five more minutes. Turning my back on the shore, I push forward, lifting my reluctant chilled arms, willing them to move. The going is slow, my timing harder to find now my body is clumsy with cold.

With brutal suddenness, something lungs at me under the water, knocking me sideways. Then I'm flailing about, my feet searching for the bottom, but I'm in too deep. I swallow water, choking and gasping, the bitterness scouring my throat as my bruised body sings in protest. Recovering myself, still reeling, I look around frantically. My heart dives. A dark shape is arcing back under the water, approaching me rapidly.

I spin around, hoping to swim in a different direction, and there's another dark streak. Uh-oh. Make that streaks. Not one, but two shapes swimming side by side, quickly closing the gap between us. I'm surrounded again, outnumbered for the second time in a few hours. And this time I don't know who or what's coming for me. The water churns with my frantic efforts to escape, but my first attacker reaches me again in an effortless glide. Something brushes against my side, more gently this time, jostling my arm.

The other two are right behind, charging toward me. I don't cry out, and now of course, when no one could blame me, I don't fall apart. There's no time to do anything but brace myself for the impact.

It might be nothing but a childhood fantasy, but I'm perfect superhero material. Absent parent, check. Social awkwardness, check. A passable body for head-to-toe lycra, check. All I'm missing is a freak accident or strange encounter. And maybe this is it.

As if I could be that lucky.

I have to face it—I'm no superhero. My body seems to agree and my mind slips into darkness a few seconds after I make one last wish for a quick and painless death.

SIX DAYS

There's gritty sand underneath me, warm from the sun. Warm from the sun, in October, in Ireland? Already I know something is very wrong, and I haven't even opened my eyes. When I do, I find I'm lying on my side in my torn salt-stained clothes on a stretch of pale sand. I can hear the gentle surge of waves close by. Moving tentatively, I test my arms and legs, but I can't find pain anywhere. Not even on my face, where there should be plenty of tender places.

I sit up, and a quick look around me confirms it. I have absolutely no clue where I am. The stunning azure sea and powdered sugar beach don't even look Irish, let alone familiar. Stretched out a few feet away from me are a group of seals, basking in the mild air. They look at me curiously but don't move, even when I stand up. I'm no marine biologist, but spending as much time as I do underwater, I recognise one of them as a common grey. The rest have colouring and markings I haven't seen before, as foreign-looking as everything else I'm trying to take in. Skirting them carefully, I walk down to the shoreline, scanning the misty horizon, trying to find a familiar landmark.

A sudden shadow appears on the ground beside my own. I spin

around, looking straight into the face of a man I swear wasn't standing there a second ago.

"You're awake."

I stumble back from my new companion. My companion with a talent for stating the obvious. Who's also practically naked, holding what looks like a furry blanket around his waist to cover his otherwise bare skin. My heart takes off in a canter. Where the hell am I? Who is this creep?

"I don't know who you are, but you can back off," I say carefully, keeping my voice steady. "Don't come any closer."

The man takes one step back, which isn't anything like far enough for me.

"Don't worry. You're safe now." Lifting his hand, the stranger holds it up, palm open. That leaves him with only one hand to hold up his dappled silver covering. It's thick and looks heavy, the weight dragging it down and revealing the whorls of hair at the base of his toned stomach. Making it obvious he isn't wearing anything underneath. Ignoring his reassurances, I put another step between us.

"Where am I?" I square my shoulders. I'm hoping to at least seem intimidating. Enough to make him think twice about whatever he's planning, dressed in that getup. "And more to the point, who are you?"

"I'm no threat to you, so don't be worrying about that," he answers, his voice smooth. "Nothing bad can happen to you here."

Wherever *here* is. The man's fur creeps further down. Let's hope he doesn't turn around and give me what I'm sure is more than a glimpse of his arse. Although judging by the rest of his body, it wouldn't be a totally unpleasant experience. If I'm able to temporarily forget he might be a kidnapper. Or worse.

He has waves of pewter hair but a youngish face, with fine lines around his cautious eyes the only sign he's probably in his mid-thirties. A dusky tan bathes his body. All over, by the look of it. A silver fox wrapped in matching fur. The effect is disconcerting. I try to stop myself from staring and my cheeks from turning crimson. Failing miserably on both counts.

His gaze is equally intense, sizing me up, making me blush deeper. "David is my name."

I deliberately don't offer him mine. "And do you think you could put on some clothes, David?"

"Afraid not. I don't have any here with me." He furrows his brow. "We didn't expect to be running into anyone so far out at sea. Then we found you in trouble."

I obviously did my dying swan act before he found me, which is why I don't remember him. But I'm safe on dry land, and someone got me here. He could be telling the truth. I look away from him reluctantly, only long enough to do a brief sweep of my surroundings. He seems to be alone. "We?"

"My friends and I."

I'm not sure if I should be more or less worried that there's no sign of them. If they're as strange as he seems to be, I'm probably better off. Unless they don't exist, and he's delusional. That might be worse.

"Where are they, then? Your friends?"

His face twitches with something like impatience. "They're here, too. On the island."

So we're on an island. At least I've found out that much. The vagueness of his answer matches his guarded look. Neither is reassuring.

"I guess I owe you a thank you," I say cautiously. "For getting me out of the water."

He dismisses my thanks with a shrug. "You called for help. So we answered."

Confusion swamps me. "I don't remember calling out." My mind flashes to the dark shapes in the water, the last thing I remember. "Something was attacking me. Did you see them?"

David frowns. "We found you alone. Alone and injured."

He's right about that one. I had been hurt. I give my body

another quick once-over. No bruises anywhere. My fingers explore my face. Both eyes are fully open, no swelling, no pain.

"And now I'm not," I say in an undertone, mystified.

One of the seals suddenly barks, catching my attention. It gives its sleek body a shake, and the penny drops with a clang.

"They were seals. That's what I saw in the water." Sweet relief washes over me. My overactive imagination has been working its magic again, turning a pod of harmless seals crossing my path into malevolent beings.

I need to stop imagining the worst all the time. I've barely finished that thought when I look more closely at Silver Fox, also known as David. And it has me imagining the worst all over again. The worst of the worst.

"Is that seal fur? Is that *a pelt*?"

David shifts his feet, looking slightly alarmed. "What?"

I move in for a closer look, my skin contracting with sudden horror. "You're a sick bastard," I explode. "It's not only kidnapping you're into, is it?"

His face turns to stone. "Kidnapping?" he asks coldly. "I hope you're not implying I kidnapped you."

"Is that why you're here? To hunt seals? Is that what you were doing when you found me?"

"You don't know how ridiculous you sound."

His cool denial while he stands there, wrapped in the evidence, makes the blood in my ears pound like battle drums.

"Says the guy wearing the sealskin. They're a protected species. Don't think I won't report you, even if you did get me out of the water."

His eyes glitter dangerously as he looks me up and down.

"If I were you," he says, his voice heavy with warning, "I would be much more careful about who I accused, and of what. I wasn't hunting them, you foolish boy."

Inside my toned athlete's body, a wary tongue-tied loner of a kid is still rattling around, and calling me a boy reminds me uncomfortably of that. His words light me up like a firecracker. I don't know what comes over me, but something snaps inside and I go for him, resigning myself to my second fight in as many days, and the first one I've ever started. I've had to stomach people abusing their power for so long—it's like suddenly, I can't swallow any more of it. But then, my timing has always been terrible, outside of the pool, anyway.

David's hands whip up and trap mine before they make contact, and his pelt thumps onto the sand. I keep my eyes on his thunderous expression.

"I don't believe you," I growl, struggling in his iron grip. Even with my new physique, I'm no match for his powerful hold. My muscles tremble under the strain of trying to break free, as the rest of me quivers with humiliation. And something else. The shivery feeling that slides down my skin from being so close to him. With fierce effort, I twist, almost wrenching myself from him.

"Lads, a little help here?" he shouts, directing his piercing glare past me.

I sense a blur of movement at the very edge of my vision, and David lets me go abruptly, making me stagger backwards. Straight into the two men suddenly standing behind me. I whirl around. Two men who also don't have any clothes on. There are two pelts puddled on the sand beside them, and only one seal is left in sight. The small grey one, who examines my shocked face with curious eyes. I'm in the middle of a naked man triangle, and nothing makes sense.

I try to push past them, but they have me surrounded. I really don't want to end up in a struggle, considering the circumstances. Free willy has just taken on a whole new meaning.

"Lads! Your pelts!" David barks out.

The one closest to me with russet hair and a friendly, open face picks up the red-brown pelt at his feet. "Whoops. Better put the old tackle away, eh?"

The other one groans and turns to me. "I apologise on his behalf, young man. For every social grace that exists, he will suffer from a lack of it. But then, he *is* a fisherman." As he stoops to retrieve the other pelt, a golden one, I see how tall he is, with pinkish skin and a lock of blond hair falling over his forehead. He looks more mature than his fisherman friend, who can't be much older than me.

David rescues his fur from the ground and takes it in a firm grip. "I told you, you're safe with us. So you need to calm down. Meet Cathal. And Oliver." He nods towards each of them in turn.

Cathal, the younger-looking one, wraps his pelt loosely around his middle. "Better?"

"Slightly." I'm wide awake, pumped full of adrenalin, but that doesn't stop me from subtly pinching myself in case I'm dreaming.

He holds out his hand. "And you are?"

"Forget the handshake. Keep both hands on your fur. *Please.* I'm Marin."

They stand there eyeing me cautiously for an uncomfortably long time until I can't bear another second of it.

"Can someone please tell me what the fuck is going on here?"

"You may as well tell him," Cathal says. "The cat's out of the bag. Or the seal's out of the pelt."

The three of them exchange glances, and Oliver nods at David.

"We're selkies," David says. "Do you know what that is?"

Selkies? I vaguely remembered a page about them in an Irish legends book I got from my school library circa 1990. Something about magical fae in seal form, who can also shed their skins and appear human. That's certainly one explanation for what I witnessed a few moments ago. Either that or I've cracked my skull and I'm probably in a coma somewhere. I can't decide which is more likely.

I give David a reluctant nod.

"Then you'll understand this is my pelt. And maybe now, you can stop trying to fight me."

"Suits me," I say airily. I press my arms to my sides to hide the slight quivering I can't shake off. "I'm not usually the fighting type."

"I could tell," he says with a slight smirk.

The grey seal watches us closely, looking bemused.

"What about you? You shy or something?" I return its stare. "Come on, let's see what you've got when your fur comes off."

Oliver, the lanky blond, gives a polite cough. "Ah, actually, that's Grey. He is, in fact, a seal."

Oh, well. It was an honest mistake.

I spin to confront David. It isn't hard to work out that he's in charge and the others defer to him. "If I'm so safe with ye, why did you attack me in the first place? Did you mistake me for a shark or something?"

"Attack you? We rescued you, boy," he says sternly.

"Don't call me boy," I snap, glaring at him. "I'm not one. And the name is Marin."

He gives a small, "whatever" toss of his head.

"If you were the seals that charged at me," I continue, "then I hate to break it to you, but that's not how you rescue someone."

"I already told you. We're not seals. We're selkies." He speaks with infuriating patience.

"I'm sorry I didn't notice the difference, when your furry arse was colliding with mine," I retort. "And I never asked for your help."

"Yes, you did."

We glower at each other.

"Let's not argue over the finer details." Oliver offers me a small, hopeful smile. "What David is trying to say is you called for assistance, and as selkies, we were obliged to answer that call. We may have answered it a little too exuberantly."

"Yeah, that sounds plausible," I agree caustically. "I said, My life can't get any worse, what I need now is some bare-arsed mermen to knock me unconscious and drag me back to their lair."

"Not mermen. *Selkies*." David's steady tone is wavering.

I raise an eyebrow. "My mistake. Maybe it was the stink of fish that confused me."

There is a slight fishy smell being carried on the sea breeze, but it isn't coming from them. They have a strong scent all right, but it makes my head spin and my guts flutter. A mixture of sea salt, caramel and wood smoke.

He gives a frustrated sigh. "We thought you were struggling," he says slowly, emphasising each word. "You were heading further and further into deep water."

"Where I come from, that's called swimming." I match his condescending tone. "I wasn't in any trouble."

David goes to cross his arms and stops himself hastily, obviously realising he needs them to maintain his modesty. He gives me a dubious look. "Then why were you crying?"

A flash of shame burns through me, making me squirm.

"Not because I was in trouble," I say shortly. Not drowning kind of trouble, anyway. I turn to Oliver, who looks to be the most sensible one and my best chance of arranging a ride home. "I wish I could stay and argue with you, but I need to get back. Urgently. So if you could tell me how I get home from wherever this is..."

David starts to speak, then hesitates. They all look guilty. More sheepish than a rack of lamb. I peer out over the jewel-like water, trying to get an idea of where I am. The horizon is clear now, and past Cathal's impressive bicep I glimpse a rocky island. My monks' rock. Then it dawns on me.

"We're on that island. The other one. The one that appeared out of nowhere."

"Not nowhere," Oliver corrects me. "This is Hy-Brasil, and it's always here. But it's only visible to your human eyes every seven years, when the mist lifts on All Hallow's Eve. And even then, only for seven days. Six days now. You were asleep for nearly twenty-four hours." He's much better at explaining things than David, with a calm matter-of-fact tone that somehow doesn't rub me up the wrong way.

"I was asleep for that long?"

"David healed your injuries. That kind of magic takes some time to wear off."

I'm not sure how I feel about David or his magic being anywhere near me while I was out of it, but I shoot him a grudging look of thanks. His eyes won't meet mine, focusing on Oliver instead as he glares at him with a shut-the-fuck-up expression.

"That's all very interesting, Oliver. But I have to get back. My mom hasn't been well, and she'll be worried about me."

"About that..." David trails off.

"What do you know about selkies?" Oliver asks hesitantly.

"That they like to walk around naked and kidnap random people from the ocean. Besides that, not a lot."

"Selkies are the souls of people who died at sea." Cathal says it casually, as if he isn't one of them. It makes me feel guilty for being less than friendly to him.

"Oh. Sorry. For your death, I mean," I stammer awkwardly.

"No bother. It was a long time ago." He shrugs.

"But thank you for your condolences, all the same." Oliver tips his head in a little bow. He is effortlessly charming. I could get used to this level of politeness.

"When the sea took our souls, it trapped us in the immortal realm, the Otherworld. But when Hy-Brasil becomes visible, for those seven days, we can roam free in the mortal world."

"I guess you're free to roam into mortals, too," I say.

David bristles, but Oliver seems to take no notice of my dig.

"And if during that time, a human calls us, our fates become intertwined."

My forehead furrows as I take in the significance of Oliver's words.

"I think I know where you're going with this. But I keep telling you, I didn't call you."

"That's where you're wrong," Cathal chimes in.

"Seven tears," Oliver says quietly. "If someone cries seven tears into the sea, during those seven days, then they summon a selkie. Creating a connection between them that neither one can sever, until this place disappears again."

"So I'm kind of tied to one of you now?"

He winces slightly, looking uncomfortable. "Evidently, it's all of us."

"All of you?" I ask, my voice rising fast. "I'm tied to *all three of you?* How?"

"You must be lucky, handsome." Cathal winks at me and Oliver shakes his head at him.

"We're not sure," David says. "It's never happened before, as far as we know. All we can think of is that you cried *a lot*." It's a shame none of Oliver's charm seems to have rubbed off on him.

"It wasn't *that* much." It's times like this I wish I could be five again, when poking out my tongue was a brutally effective and socially acceptable comeback.

"However it happened, we tied your fate to ours, and you have to remain close to us, for the time being." Oliver's face mirrors his apologetic tone.

"Are you saying I'm stuck here for *seven days?*" I'm almost yelling now.

"Six days, remember?" Cathal corrects me cheerily.

"And what if I insist you let me go?"

"Believe me, we would," David says with increasing belligerence. "But the island wouldn't let you leave. Not without us."

"Then leave with me. Take me back."

"That wouldn't be practical," Oliver explains. "We'd have to stay very close to you until the bond breaks. I'm not sure how you would explain our presence to your human companions."

Not a problem. I don't have many human companions.

"How close?" I demand.

"Very close." Cathal crosses his fingers together, quirking his eyebrows.

"So, you're refusing to take me home?"

"We're saying we can't," David says impatiently. "The week will go by before you know it, and then you'll never have to see us again. Complaining about the situation won't make it any more bearable. For you or for us."

We face off against each other, near enough to touch, digging our heels stubbornly into the warm sand, while Oliver and Cathal hover nervously around us. I look into his eyes, really look, for the first time. And just like that, the fight leaves me. Because I can't see anything. Only a kind of emptiness, as coldly indifferent as the sea he drowned in. And like him, I know I'll never win against it.

"Fine," I say coolly. "Let me know when you're all about to disappear again. In the meantime, stay the hell away from me."

Whirling around, I take off at a marching pace, not stopping until I'm out of their sight. I stumble down to the edge of the delicate ruffled waves and stared out over the water. Its surface is impossibly calm. The opposite of me at that moment.

I seem to be spending way too much time staring out over large bodies of water, reflecting on everything wrong with my life. At least I don't feel like crying, because that's what got me into this mess. My eyes are hot and dry, my body a burning coal of resentment.

With a sudden burst of energy, I wade out and plunge headfirst into the water. I push myself hard, making rapid progress, my steady rhythm carrying me away from the shore. I'll get home on my own steam if I have to. I can head for my monks' rock first, where I can rest before beginning the last wearying leg home. But about twenty metres out I vibrate all over with sudden shock, my body ricocheting backwards like I've run up against an invisible brick wall. I spend a good half-hour pushing against it, trying to circle it, which leaves me with nothing but sore muscles and a matching temper.

Coasting back to the beach, I slump onto the sand. After taking some time to calm down, I'm willing to admit the island may have done me a favour by refusing to let me go. I'd never survive that swim if I tried it. Even I'm not used to that distance, not without proper backup. I lean back and shut out the view. Maybe I can sleep for six days. It's worth a try.

21

"You hungry?"

I open a wary eye to Cathal bending over me, a fish in his hand. He's looped his pelt over one shoulder and tied it with a long strand of dune grass.

"I like the caveman look," I say, my voice bitter with sarcasm.

"David's orders. No more flashing the guest." He grins. "Do you like fish?" He thrusts it out towards me, and I grimace.

"I like *cooked* fish."

His face flushes. "Sorry. It's been a while. I forgot that little human detail."

"I'm not sure having to cook flesh is a little detail, but don't worry, I forgive you." I feel bad about making *him* feel bad. I have to admit, he's an agreeable sort of guy. As weird magical sea creatures go.

"Look, I'm the one who should be apologising, for being so rude to you. It's nothing personal. I'm only anxious to get back home."

"Were you rude? I didn't notice. It's the thick skin," he answers with an easy smile.

Gathering some smooth black stones from the surrounding sand, he piles them into a circle. He mutters something, and a second later they start to steam. The fish sizzles when he throws it onto the rocks.

"That's impressive."

"I have my moments. One advantage of being a selkie. It comes with a bit of fae magic. Not as much as the gods, but enough to do a few party tricks." He bounces his eyebrows up and down, his teeth flashing in another sudden smile. Flopping down beside me, he digs his toes in until they disappear into the sand.

"David asked me to feed you, but I wanted to find you, anyway. There's something you should know. He's too noble to tell you, but I say it's better if you know from the start what the deal is with us."

"I thought Oliver filled me in already?"

His smile dies. "That one is too polite for his own good." He shakes his head. "No. David and Oliver told you *a* story. They didn't tell you the whole story."

"So? Don't leave me in suspense." I lean forward, secretly inhaling the scent of him, sweet and salty. Taking up a stick, he pokes at the fish as its skin blackens and shrivels.

"Oliver told you about these seven days when we can roam free in your world. But there's something else that becomes possible for a selkie every seven years. It's rare, but it happens. And that's finding a human mate."

"Doesn't give you much of a window, does it? One week, every seven years? But you're not an unattractive guy. Although you could try putting some clothes on." I'm increasingly aware of his powerful leg close to mine, and my pulse quickens. "On second thought, maybe not."

He ignores my joking, his expression remaining solemn. "It has to be someone who called us."

The implication isn't lost on me. I take a deep breath, trying to hold it together.

"So, I'm thinking, me," I say slowly.

"Got it in one." His golden eyes search my face anxiously.

"Well, I know you're probably a bit out of the loop, being a mythical being stuck on an island that doesn't exist, but these days, consent is a thing. No more fairy tale kisses while you're unconscious or having your destiny decided by pissed-off fairies."

"Oh, you have to consent," he assures me. "It's your decision if you choose to break the unbreakable bond."

"So, not actually unbreakable, then?"

His mouth twists in a wry smile. "No."

I give a small and what I hope is discreet sigh of relief. "How about I speed the process up and let you out of your contract right now?"

"If that were possible, you can bet David would have suggested it. I told you, he didn't even want you to find out about the whole human mate thing."

"I wonder why," I say drily.

"It's not like that. He wasn't happy about putting that sort of pressure on you."

"Yeah. I'm sure that's the reason."

Cathal chuckles. "You'll still have to wait it out, I'm afraid. Six days. And 'tis a special situation. More complicated than the usual." He takes another large stone from the sand, brushing it down and flipping the fish onto it before handing it to me.

"How so?"

"Because somehow you called three of us. So if you do decide you want to be bonded to one of us forever, you're going to have to choose between us."

I take a small piece of fish, playing for time so I can summon some tact.

"You seem like a great guy, Cathal, but it won't come to that. I can't stay, anyway. My mom needs me. And even if she didn't, I don't think this place is for me."

"You wouldn't have to stay in the Otherworld. A bonded selkie is free. To come and go from both realms, always. Your mate could go anywhere with you."

I'm not sure how to respond, biding my time. For a few seconds, I allow myself to imagine I'm not alone, to feel what it would be like to arrive back in Seafort with someone like Cathal beside me.

What am I thinking? Someone like Cathal? A mythical creature who eats raw fish and walks around naked? I doubt Seafort is ready for that.

I suddenly grin at the thought, which only seems to encourage him.

"You'll come around," he beams. "Eventually. I'm an acquired taste."

"Like raw fish," I counter smartly.

He laughs, a deep musical sound, like bells ringing. "I don't smell as bad."

"Are you sure about that, ancient mythical one?" I poke him

gently in the ribs. Despite myself, I can't help liking him, even if he did kidnap me. I sigh again. I can't see this ending well.

"I'm not ancient," he corrects me. "What year is it?"

"It's 1997. October. Or November, now."

"Then I'm nearly fifty. I'll have to throw a party. A combined one for my thirtieth and my fortieth..."

"Are you telling me you were born in 1947?"

"Last day of the year, baby."

"You don't look fifty."

"It's all those seawater baths," he jokes. "So tell me, did the Beatles get back together? I was gutted when they broke up."

"You mean you died before... um, no, they didn't. Someone shot John Lennon."

"Fuck me! He's dead?"

I nod reluctantly. He sits there in subdued silence for a few minutes before his eyes light up again. "What about the Grateful Dead? I saved all my pennies and caught the boat to London to see them on tour, right before I died. Amazing, they were."

"They're more like the dead Dead these days. Jerry Garcia is anyway. He died a couple of years ago, I think."

"Ah, no." His face falls, and he gives a small shrug. "Ah, well. Join the club, Jerry. Happens to all of us. And he got a bit longer than I did. I was only twenty-four." He manages a muted smile, making me feel terrible, my arms itching to give him a comforting hug. There's something kind of adorable about his infectious good humour that refuses to quit, even while I'm brutally killing off his heroes one by one.

"I shouldn't have told you." I put the fish down and rest a tentative hand on his arm. He's firm, all hard muscle, and his skin radiates warmth like trapped sunlight. My insides flip in appreciation. "Dying is the last thing you need to hear about."

"Don't be troubling yourself, buachaill," he says, soothing me with his musical voice. For some reason, I don't seem to mind at all when *he's* the one calling me a boy. "I got swept off a fishing trawler.

25

Could happen to anyone." One of his large hands closes over mine. "Tell me, what made you cry?"

My heart dives as I remember. "Not what. Who. His name's Kevin."

"Is he your... you know... your lover?" he asks shyly.

"Jesus, no! Just your common everyday arsehole."

Snorting with sudden laughter he leans forward, touching his forehead gently to mine, a spike of his hair flopping down to brush my face, his breath soft on my skin. I lean back, startled, snatching my hand away and trying to ignore the effect of his sudden closeness on my cock.

"I think you may have got the wrong idea." My breaths are more than a little shaky. "I wasn't trying to start something. I was feeling bad for you, that's all."

He shifts away slightly, looking confused.

"Sorry, Marin. It's only, I..." His eyes drop to the sand. "I've never been with a lad before. I never expected one to be calling me. And now I'm fecking clueless about how it's supposed to go. I wasn't sure if you wanted me to make a move, or what."

He has a way of disarming me without even trying.

"I'm surprised," I mock him gently. "I've heard some stories about fishermen. All those long, lonely nights at sea."

He looks up again, his smile returning. "Don't believe everything you hear." He gives a brazen wink. "Not *all* of it. Of course, those stories are true. But not in my case. Not because I'm against the idea," he adds hastily. "I had a girlfriend, and that's all I knew. As for being with a lad, it never came up." He gets more and more flustered. "I mean..."

I smile at his discomposure, although I try to hide it. "I know what you mean."

We sit silently for a minute, while I wrestle with what to share and what to keep to myself. But his guilelessness and honesty make me want to meet him somewhere in the middle.

"I haven't really been with a guy, either," I mutter.

His surprise is obvious. He's sort of an open book. Not like my locked-up diary of secrets. "I thought you were—"

"Gay? Or whatever you called it in the swinging sixties? I am," I tell him. "I've only ever been attracted to guys. But there wasn't any opportunity to act on it where I grew up. And then I moved somewhere else where there was almost too much opportunity. I felt a bit overwhelmed. Shy."

Funnily enough, that's exactly how I'm feeling now. I sense Cathal's eyes still on me as I avert mine, looking out over the water. The silence drags on while I struggle to think of some way to change the subject until my gaze latches onto the rocky triangle on the horizon.

"You know, I've always wanted to go there." I nod towards it. "But you have to have a special permit. It used to be a monastic settlement, but it's a wildlife reserve these days."

"Well, I'm wildlife," he says with a flashing grin. "We can go if you like. We can go anywhere we want for the next few days, and the lads and I always take advantage of it. Although we stay away from humans, as much as we can. We've been this way for so long that we don't know how to act around them anymore. But, why there?"

"Because it's peaceful. And quiet. And far away from everyone else."

He chuckles. "You may be in for a shock. All the islands in the mortal realm will be overrun with selkies for the next few days, looking to enjoy their few days of freedom. Maybe even hoping for a bit of human bonding." His eyes twinkle. "That's one thing I won't have to worry about. For the first time, I got the call." His voice is deep and soft, husky and inviting. His hand finds mine where it rests in the sand, and one of his fingers traces a delicate circle on the back of it.

It sends my heart galloping faster, shivers tickling my neck as my ears buzz with a rush of blood. My whole body is spinning with the sudden vertigo of want, and this time my swelling cock is difficult to ignore. I'm not the only one aware of it. Cathal's eyes drop to my trousers fleetingly, before his gaze catches and holds mine. He stares at me with a knowing expression, his face suddenly serious, and all at once, I'm struggling to get my breath. I'm so tempted to kiss him, and it's not like I have to marry him afterwards. I've got six days to kill, and this is one way to make them go faster.

"First time for everything," I murmur shyly.

He hesitates, looking at me earnestly. "Am I right in thinking that you wouldn't mind if I... I'm not sure I'm reading the signals right... but I'm getting the feeling that you—"

"For feck's sake kiss me you eejit, before I change my mind."

His lips barely brush mine before he pauses and pulls away, examining me closely. Even that brief touch is enough to send sparks zipping up my nerve endings. My lips chase after his, and I stop his retreat by looping my fingers gently around his warm, tanned neck. There's nothing tentative about my answering kiss. As he opens up to me, I explore the sweet heat of his mouth with my tongue, and he tastes as good as he smells, a mix of brine and burnt toffee.

I melt into the warm sand, my pulse singing, and my other hand runs down his silky pelt. But when it brushes his hard cock, pushing against the soft fur, all of a sudden I'm confused and uncertain. It's all very well to give in to the moment, but that's all it can be. A moment. I *want* Cathal to keep kissing me. To touch me the way I'm touching him. Fuck, there are no words to describe how much I want it. And that's the trouble, because I can't want it this badly. There's no point in starting anything that might be hard to stop. I *need* to get back to reality and sort out my life.

A sharp bark startles me, and I jump, turning to face the sound. Grey is a few paces down the beach, gazing at us with a look I can only describe as disapproving.

With a shuddering sigh, I release Cathal and lean back. He regards me cautiously, his eyes concerned.

"All right, lad?"

I nod, reassuring him with my smile, and he answers with a relieved grin.

"What about you? All right?"

"Never been better. So, come here to me... was that the first time you kissed a fella?"

In Berlin, even with my nerves and inexperience, I got as far as kissing, and even further. That's when I knew for sure it was what I wanted. Because it felt amazing. Right. And this does too, and then some. Many times more amazing.

My sudden awkwardness is leaving me, making me brave enough to lean forward and rest my forehead on his, just like he'd done to me earlier. Our noses almost touching, I answer him.

"No. But it was the first time I kissed a selkie."

He gives a delighted laugh, sending his sweet breath puffing onto my cheek. "I'll take it."

Grey gives another bark. Breaking apart, we look up to find he's crept closer, only metres away from us. Cathal jumps up and rushes at him with an exasperated grimace, waving his arms.

"Shoo, Grey, you nosey creature! Go spy on someone else." Grey gives him one last look with his big eyes before he obediently shuffles to the water's edge and launches himself into the sea.

I narrow my eyes. "Are you sure he's not one of you?"

"I hope not. I've got enough competition as it is," Cathal complains. "But I think I'm a few lengths ahead in this race. Excuse the pun."

I burn as I colour up. "I told you. There is no race." I rustle up the most discouraging look I can manage. So far, I've failed pretty miserably when it comes to keeping him and his enthusiasm at bay.

"Whatever you say. I think I might saddle up, anyway. You never know."

As he stands over me with a brash smile, I'm conscious of his erection under his pelt, and how close it is to my face. And what I'd like to do to it. And what I'd like it to do to me. He catches me looking and winks, long and slow. Another sudden flush of heat sends me shivering, and his grin disappears.

"You're cold," he says, full of concern. "Here, take my pelt."

He rips off the grass that binds it and slips it off, turning so he isn't revealing too much as he holds it out to me.

"What David doesn't see can't be hurting him. You won't be telling on me, will you?" When I don't reach out to take it, he sobers, looking at me carefully. "Marin, I was only messing with you. I'll keep a respectable distance, I promise. No more funny business. Just take it."

The fur slides warm and weighty into my hands, and he helps me wrap it around my shoulders. He settles himself so he's sitting behind me, his back firm against mine.

"This way I can keep you warm, without getting myself too, er, overheated," he says, a hint of teasing laughter in his voice.

I force myself to stop quaking, leaning back into him. I'm glad he can't see my conflicted feelings laid bare. Cathal isn't the only one who needs to cool down. If I'm going to get through this week with no complications, it's not a good idea to let anything else happen between us. And it's definitely better if he doesn't see how disappointed I am about that.

FIVE DAYS

I wake up cosy and warm, something soft but substantial pressing on my body. Blinking, I move to get up, and it slides off me. I look more closely, and I remember. Cathal's pelt. He's sitting closer to the shore, staring out at the horizon, and it strikes me again how muscular and powerful his body is. As I approach him, he stands up and turns around, beaming. I try to keep my eyes on his face and fail miserably. Hmm. So he's powerful and muscular all over, then. He's a redhead all over too, his body hair the same russet-brown as his spiky locks.

"Ah, good. I was waiting for you to get your arse up, so I could go fishing." If he sees my sneaky peeking, he's chivalrous enough to ignore it.

I don't remember falling asleep. Yesterday we talked for a long time, long after the light left us. I found out he was from a village not far south of Seafort, although I didn't know his family. We spent a lot of the time comparing notes, and childhoods. His had been very different from mine, but not any easier. He'd been a deckhand on his brother's trawler since he was fourteen. No chance of escaping on a

31

scholarship like me. Only endless nights of brutally hard work before he plunged into the unforgiving ocean.

It was easy to talk in the dark. Now I can see his friendly face, some of my awkwardness returns, hyper-aware of how my body is responding to the sight of his.

"Did I sleep with your pelt all night?"

"That's the only part of me you slept with, don't worry. I'm caught up with this consent thing now. Welcome to the nineties, Cathal Moran."

He scoops up the pelt and looks at me, doubt flitting across his face.

"You might want to give this a miss, seeing me shift. 'Tis a bit more shocking than seeing me butt naked. Strange enough to watch, the first time." He points farther down the beach. "There's a fresh-water stream running into the ocean, in from the dunes there, if you want to get cleaned up. You must smell like a seal after spending a night under my fur."

"Are you joking? If I could bottle your scent, I'd never have to work, or live in Seafort, or deal with people like Kevin. Ever again."

Cathal breaks into a grin, obviously delighted with the compliment.

"After you freshen up, Oliver's in the next cove. He'd love a chat with you. He misses intelligent conversation. I'm a dead loss, so he says."

I leave him and walk along the shoreline, letting the sun-warmed sea caress my feet. This island seems to have its own microclimate. After finding the stream without any trouble, I take the time to wash properly, removing several layers of sand and sea salt. I wash everything I'm wearing too, although my trousers will never recover their former shiny glory, and my shirt is hopelessly creased. My clothes and hair dry in no time in the warm wind. And the waters of this place are obviously as magical as the inhabitants. My locks are silky smooth after their thorough soaking, and my skin practically glows.

Back on the beach, I see Oliver's tall frame in line with my own as he wanders along the shoreline, stooping down to gather something and then straightening up again. I approach him, adjusting my face to what I hope is a friendly smile. He isn't wearing anything either, his pelt in an untidy pile next to him. I don't mind. I can't expect them to carry those things around for the rest of the week. This time I don't even bother trying to disguise my curiosity as I take in the sight of him. He's lithe and firm, all lean contours and pale glistening skin.

As I get close to him, he reaches out and takes one of my hands. His fingers are slim and delicate, and noticeably soft. Opening up my hand gently, he places something on my palm. It's a shimmering stone, shaped like a droplet, woven through with blue and green.

"What is it?" I ask, stunned by how beautiful it is. The sun finds it, and streaks of aquamarine play over my calloused hand.

"Mermaids' tears. That's what they're called. They're all over the island." He takes his hand away, his pale cheeks reddening.

"And, are they? Made from mermaids' tears, I mean?"

He shakes his head. "Of course not. That's nonsense. There's some geological explanation for their appearance. There's no such thing as mermaids."

"You're a mythical creature who doesn't believe in another mythical creature."

He gives a soft self-conscious laugh, almost like a cough. "You have a point. It's the man of science in me. Once an anthropologist, always one. Even after being transformed into a mythical shapeshifter."

"Is that what you were? An anthropologist?" My hand closes over the stone and its trapped warmth pulses against my palm. Beside me, Oliver frowns, his face thoughtful.

"Yes. From Bristol. Social anthropology was my chief area of interest. I was here for five years, studying the local traditions of that island you see over there. I recorded all the myths and legends, including the ones about selkies." He gives a small smile. "I suppose you could say I went to great lengths to uncover irrefutable proof of their existence. It's a great pity I couldn't share my findings with my university colleagues. Of course, they're all dead. Many years."

"How long?"

"My study began in 1892. As I said. A long time." He lets out a whispering sigh as his eyes meet mine. They're deep green, paler than mermaids' tears, but just as startling.

"What about you, Marin? What is your passion?"

I'm not used to talking about myself, but Oliver's gaze is warm and interested. Something about his quiet sincerity makes me feel special, singled out, like there's a spotlight shining on me, making the rest of the world fade into the background. He gives a little nod, encouraging me.

"I guess it's swimming. I won a European scholarship to spend a few years training in Germany. But I had to give it up and come home. My mom's been sick. She's a lot better now, but I wanted to give her a break. Take care of things for a while."

"You mentioned that. I'm dreadfully sorry to hear it." There's genuine regret in his voice. His sudden chuckle is as quiet and unassuming as the rest of him.

"It is amusing when you think of it though, isn't it?" he asks. "We came rushing in to rescue an expert swimmer. We certainly misjudged that situation."

I can join him in smiling about it now. Almost. "You really did. I only got into trouble *after* one of you cannoned into me."

"That was David. I've never seen him so frantic. I think that's why he misjudged his speed when he approached you." Oliver creases his forehead again. "And then you passed out, and he panicked and brought you back here. And we never bring mortals here. It's not strictly forbidden, but not exactly encouraged. It was very much out of character. He's usually so measured."

"If by measured, you mean an uptight pain in the arse, then my first impression was right," I say shortly. "What's his deal, anyway?"

Oliver sniffs the air. "Cooked fish. Now there's a novelty. For your benefit, I'm assuming. Let's walk back towards Cathal, and I'll tell you." Picking up his pelt, he swings it over one shoulder.

"Thank you for not commenting on my general state of undress, by the way," he adds, as we make our way along the beach, side by side.

"No bother. I'm enjoying it. I might even walk behind you for a while, to get more of the rear view." I surprise myself by being brave enough to wink at him, and he blushes pink again.

"I'm only familiar with Victorians, and they're not quite so uninhibited," he remarks. "Things must have changed a lot since I was last in the mortal world."

"Walking around naked will still get you arrested," I inform him. "But this is your place, so your rules, I guess. I'm good with it. Now tell me about David."

He doesn't answer immediately, stopping to scoop up another shimmering mermaid's tear and skim it expertly along the surface of the water.

"He's a good man, Marin. He's had the worst of it in many ways. He tried to save his son from drowning, and he couldn't. At least I never had guilt to make my death worse, as he did. When David lost his soul to the sea, I was the one who protected him and taught him our ways. Then when Cathal came, David was his protector. Cathal is so reckless he needs lots of protecting, as you can imagine."

I certainly can. "But who protected you, in the beginning?"

"When I first became what I am now, I had a much older selkie who looked after me. He stayed with me for a long time. There were four of us, for a little while, after Cathal came." He starts walking again, concentrating hard on his feet. "Afterwards, David took over many of his responsibilities. Leadership doesn't sit comfortably with me. David's much more of a natural at it."

"And the other selkie, your old leader. What happened to him?"

Looking up at me, his eyes narrow, pain slipping across his face before he recovers. "He died."

"So, you're not immortal?" A few days ago I didn't believe in mythical creatures. Now my heart is aching for one of them.

"We live until something or someone mortally wounds us. That could take two hundred years, or two thousand. So immortal, no. But technically, it's possible, if we stay out of trouble. It's easier for some of us than others." His lips twitch.

"Why do I think you're talking about Cathal?"

He laughs, louder this time. Taking the top of my arm, he halts my progress.

"Cathal is the youngest of us. He's a baby, for all intents and purposes, compared to David or myself."

I can agree with that. "He is pretty immature for a fifty-year-old. And these days, that's saying a lot."

Oliver's green eyes find mine again, and his smile disappears.

"I know Cathal told you everything," he says. "That boy couldn't keep his mouth shut if his very life depended upon it. And you should know that he has the most chance of adjusting to the mortal world again. That's why, if you choose to bond with any one of us, the logical decision is for you to choose him."

An unruly lock of hair, pale blond, swings over his eyes, and he looks so artless and vulnerable that my fierce protective instincts spring into action. I can't stop it. It's the Leo in me.

"Are you always so self-sacrificing, so noble?" I ask curiously.

"Only sometimes. Not always," he says with the ghost of a smile. "And not at all in this case. I simply know Cathal would make you happy. And I couldn't."

"Why do you think that?"

"Because I'm dead inside, Marin. I have the heart of a corpse. Figuratively as well as literally."

I place my hand softly on his smooth pale chest, finding the thud of his rapid pulse.

"It seems in pretty good shape to me."

"It's still capable of mechanical functions," he says grimly. "It's not capable of more than that."

"I don't believe you." I don't take my hand away, letting it rest on his cool skin. "I can feel what a good person you were. Are. How much you care about things."

"I like to think I've kept my humanity," he explains. "My basic common decency. But you don't need emotions for that." He notices my cynical expression. "You don't believe me? You couldn't get me to feel anything, as much as you might try."

His calm resignation is almost painful to me, infuriating, and my stubbornness kicks in. "All right."

"All right, what?"

"Let's try it."

He frowns. "I wasn't seriously suggesting it."

"But I am."

"Absolutely not," he says firmly.

"What are you afraid of, if you're so sure you're right?"

I'm sure he's going to keep resisting, but he surprises me with a sudden shrug. "If you insist. Try it and you'll realise what a cold fish I am."

My mermaid's tear drops to the sand as I swing my arms around his neck, bringing his face close to mine while his pelt slides to the ground. I plant a gentle kiss on the underside of his chin and he bends his head to meet mine. His arms circle me, wrapping me in a soft embrace. I imagine that's what it would be like to have a guardian angel fold their wings around me. If they existed. And after the last couple of days, I can't rule anything out.

His kiss, when it comes, is hesitant, searching. I respond enthusiastically, my lips firm on his, but he breaks away almost immediately, releasing me. He lifts my chin with a gentle finger.

"You can't take it personally that I don't respond to you. It's not any fault of yours."

"I thought you were a man of science. That was hardly a rigorous investigation. I want to see some definitive proof."

"You're not easily dissuaded, are you? Very well," he says softly. "As long as you promise not to be disappointed."

This time I kiss him, hard, permitting myself to get carried by the rising tide of feeling, hoping to sweep him away with me. My tongue pursues his, finding and claiming it while my fingers tangle in his hair. It isn't long before my cock is pressing throbbing and urgent against his bare skin. Sliding my hands from his neck, I glide them down his chest to circle his waist and rest on the curves of his arse.

He starts, but he doesn't pull away. I'm giddy with want, aching to squeeze his firm cheeks and grind myself against his lean body. But I hold it together, focusing on his tongue in my mouth and his slightly shaky hands on my hips as the minutes tick by.

Gradually, I notice a shift in his desire, as slowly he takes control. There's genuine enthusiasm in his kisses now. And passion. His cock is hardening, rubbing against me. His hands leave my hips, roaming up under my shirt, gliding along my back and down to my arse. With firm fingers, he grabs it through my trousers without any of my hesitation. All at once, the shy diffident Oliver disappears, replaced by a man who knows exactly what I want, and how to make it happen. I wish I shared his calm certainty, to know without question what to do. I'm all over the place, weak with need and terrified by the possibility of satisfying it. Pulling my mouth away from his, I stop to graze the tender skin at the base of his neck with my lips, feeling the soft groan rumble deep in his throat.

"What were you saying?" I mumble into his neck. "Something about a cold fish?"

He gives a shaky chuckle and releases me, his green eyes wide and dark with desire.

"Was that some kind of trick?" I ask breathlessly. "To get me to kiss you?"

His horrified expression is all the answer I need. "I promise you, I wasn't expecting that to happen. It never has before. Not since I became a selkie."

"It's okay," I say quickly, "I didn't think that of you." I do a slow and deliberate sweep of his body and his obvious arousal.

"So, you still think I should choose Cathal?" I ask brashly.

"Of course," he answers without hesitation. "You may have rean- imated my corpse, Victor Frankenstein, but Cathal remains the only sensible choice." Picking up his pelt, he slings it around his waist, covering himself. "You're both young. Energetic. Impulsive. Not easily discouraged."

"Stubborn?" I demand.

"If you say so." He arches his eyebrows, giving me a knowing smile.

A piercing scream shakes me, echoing in my head, leaving me shuddering with sudden pain. I clap my hands over my ears, but the wailing increases, echoing in the very air. Oliver's face crumples, his soft cheeks turning deathly grey.

"What is it?" I choke out. "What's that sound?"

"It's the selkie distress call. For mortal danger. We have to find the others." He takes my arm firmly, grasping his pelt in the other hand, and together we sprint along the beach, keeping to the shore- line where the sand is firmer.

"Is it Cathal and David?" My heart plummets at the thought. David might be a miserable bastard, but I wouldn't wish mortal danger on him. And as for Cathal...

The cries of distress turn my blood to ice, suffocating me with the heaviness of total dread.

"No, not their calls. And it's further away," he pants. Skidding to a sudden stop, he looks at me, puzzled. "Wait. You can hear them?"

"Of course I can," I say, impatient. "They're screaming, and not exactly softly."

He bites his lip and his brow creases.

"Well, never mind. Make haste!" He starts running again, pulling me along with him.

Cathal comes into view, dashing flat out, his pelt bouncing off his shoulders, his muscled legs working hard. David is ahead of us, peering grimly out to sea, and Cathal reaches him before we do. We rush up to them, breathing heavily.

"It's coming from Tasket Island," David says. "We can't waste another minute. Oliver, you come with me. Cathal, you stay here with Marin."

"No!" Cathal flares. "'Tis madness to go without me. Can't you hear that? There's something terrible happening there."

"Someone has to stay with Marin." David is calm and firm, his jaw stubborn, his voice like steel.

"No, they don't. I'll be fine. Just go. Save them." The screams have reached a fever pitch in my head, tormenting me.

"You're bonded to us, remember?" David snaps. "At least one of us has to stay with you."

"Well, whose fault is that?" My voice is prickly with resentment. "I didn't ask to be tied to any of you."

"We don't have time for this discussion," Oliver says urgently.

"It's simple. I'll come with you. Then you can all go." I lift my chin and face David. His eyes are as grey as his hair. And his personality.

"Not a chance," he spits back. "You'll be a danger to yourself and a danger to us."

I start to argue, but he grabs my wrist roughly and yanks me close to him. What was I saying about not wanting anything to happen to him? I'm bitterly rethinking that earlier statement.

"I can hear selkies dying." His words hum low but vicious in my ear. "Your bond with us means nothing compared to them. You mean nothing. For your own sake, you'll stay here with Cathal until we get back."

He lets go of me abruptly, and I almost flinch when Cathal slings a comforting arm around me. He holds me while Oliver and David dive into the water. Their pelts wrap around them, engulfing them, and they change, shifting, taking on their new form. Cathal was right, it's strange, but I've seen so much strange stuff these last couple of days that it isn't anything I can't handle. In their selkie forms, Oliver's fur is sandy, David's a deep mottled grey. They spear through the water, speeding far away from us in minutes, while the screams of the selkies scrape my mind and frustration and rage curdle my stomach.

FOUR DAYS

It's still dark, the moon shining pale in the pre-dawn sky when I stir to find Cathal curled up beside me. Oliver's face, twisted with anguish, looms over us.

"Marin. Cathal. David asked me to fetch you. Come."

His urgent words rouse Cathal and with one look at Oliver, he's jumping up and making for the water. I tilt my head, listening. The screams have stopped. All afternoon and into the night, Cathal and I huddled together, barely speaking, the unrelenting cries leaving us exhausted, longing for a reprieve. Now the silence is heavy, almost worse.

Oliver extends his hand and pulls me up.

"Oliver? Is everything—"

He shakes his head, his eyes glistening.

"You'll see for yourself. Don't worry. The danger has passed." He forces the words out as if saying each one is like swallowing a sword.

Cathal has already shifted, a reddish-brown streak of solid muscle and fur darting below the surface of the water.

Oliver examines me. "Can you swim alongside us? I'll assist you."

"Of course. Let's go."

In seconds we're in the water. Cathal skims beside me and I grab his fur while Oliver, ever the gentleman, transforms out of my range of sight. Then he's swimming alongside me, and I hold them both firmly, balancing myself between them as we rocket through the water.

I hope he can hold on. They're Cathal's thoughts. And I can hear them.

Don't underestimate him, Oliver responds. *He knows what he's doing. He's a swimmer.*

And I can hear you. So don't be talking about me as if I'm not here. I send the thought out to both of them, and I sense their recoil of shock and surprise. Looks like they can hear my thoughts too.

You can hear us? Cathal can't hide his amazement, even in his thoughts.

Obviously, I shoot back. *Let's go. Swim faster.*

I always imagined my monks' rock to be peaceful and quiet. But not this sort of quiet. The deathly kind. Because nothing lives on it—not anymore.

I'm not sure what hurts the most. Maybe the tormented cry that rips out of Cathal when he takes in the carnage and the blood. Or a grim David, rigid with grief but refusing to betray himself, as he piles the bodies up on top of the driftwood in a makeshift pyre.

I think it might be Oliver, pale and quiet, standing over one small body in particular, the waves lapping it gently, its bright blood seeping into the ocean, clouding the surface. I go to join him and it's Grey. Yeah. That's the worst part.

The pain splits me in two and I drop to my knees. My dramatics embarrass me, but that doesn't mean I have the power to stop them. It makes no sense. A few days ago, I didn't even know selkies existed. Now, I feel every bit of their suffering like a thousand cuts to my skin.

Oliver kneels beside me, gripping my shoulders firmly, humming soothing sounds in my ear.

"The ones that died. Are they selkies or seals?" I whisper.

"Both. About twenty seal pups and five selkies." Oliver leans forward to rest his head in the curve of my shoulder, and I hear the tears in his ragged breathing. "They were our friends. Two were older than me."

"But who would do this?"

"We don't know. All we know is that we were too late. David and I have been up all night, trying to save them. But his bit of healing magic was no use with injuries this severe. It was hopeless."

Pounding footsteps approach and Cathal stands over us. He sees Grey and moans, his face mottled with disbelief and grief. Then he's gone, moving towards the bloodied water with grim purpose.

"They can't be far," he throws over his shoulder.

"Cathal, stop!" Letting go of my shoulders, Oliver jumps to his feet. "What can you possibly do? Do you want the same thing to happen to you?"

Cathal pauses, up to his knees in the surf. "I'll be careful. We need to know who did this. I promise I'll stay back. I won't do anything stupid."

David comes rushing up behind us.

"Cathal. No. I forbid it. Stay here," he commands.

"I'm fifty years old. Or near enough. I'm not your pet seal, David. I'm not Grey. I'm done taking your orders." Cathal plunges deep into the tainted water, out of sight.

It's been hours, and Cathal hasn't come back. This island is in my world, not protected by any magic, and it's like any other November day. In other words, freezing. Oliver lights a fire with the same trick Cathal used earlier, and I huddle in front of it as David and Oliver pace and worry, checking the horizon every five minutes.

I spy a shape cutting through the water, the light catching its rapid progress. I call to Oliver. "Is that Cathal? Coming back?"

Oliver peers out, hope lighting up his face, but only for a second.

"That's not Cathal," he says. "It's Ré."

There's a sudden churning disturbance under the surface, and a young woman rears up out of the water, wrapping a shining white pelt around herself. It's so long it reaches her feet. Her hair is a deep glistening brown, shot through with purple, and she moves with an easy grace as she walks onto the rocky shore.

"Ray. That's her name? As in ray, a drop of shining sun?"

Oliver looked puzzled. Of course, he missed The Sound of Music and the Von Trapp family shenanigans by a good seventy years.

"Ré as in Réalta Dubh, Dark Star. Our leader."

"She looks very young to be a leader," I observe.

He gives a grim smile. "You should know by now you can't judge a selkie's age by their looks. She's the oldest selkie in existence."

She sweeps past us, moving to greet David as he stands on higher ground, some distance away. They talk for a long time, while Oliver and I crouch by the fire, watching them nervously. At one point they seem to disagree, their voices rising, and I hear Cathal's name being spoken. And maybe my own. With Ré's back to us, I notice her pelt has a black star spreading dramatically over the shining silvery white fur. Eventually, Oliver springs up with a start.

"Get ready to bow. She's coming this way."

She glides over, her pelt trailing behind her, and Oliver inclines his pale head. She gives a brief nod. This close, her fierce wildness is so magnetic and intoxicating, I feel like bowing isn't enough. I want to collapse at her feet.

"No need for all the ceremony," she says impatiently. Her voice is as musical as Cathal's and as refined as Oliver's. "Could you leave us for a moment, Oliver?" With an encouraging look at me, he goes to join David at the pyre.

"I'm sorry you had to witness all this pain, young Marin." Her snapping brown eyes bore through me, but they glow with more warmth than the fire. "David told me about you. You called three, instead of one. That's never happened in my lifetime, and since I'm as old as the first selkie, that means it's never happened at all." She's unsmiling, but not exactly unfriendly. I can't quite tell if I've managed to please or upset her with my uniqueness.

"Are you confident you'll make the right choice, deciding between the boys?" she presses me. I almost smile at the thought of David ever being a boy. It's hard to imagine. But I suppose to someone this ancient, everyone else must seem like a bratty teenager.

I wish I could give her an answer. In the last day or so, I've gone from *Hell, no* to *What if?* And every minute I spend with them makes my choice that much harder.

She tilts her head, looking at me intently. "Sometimes, Marin, the best choice is not to make one."

Does she not want me to be with any of them? A couple of days ago, I would have heartily agreed with her; now her interference riles me. "Are you telling me I should walk away?" I demand.

"I can't tell you to do anything," she says evenly. "Because then it wouldn't be your choice."

She leaves me without a goodbye, waving to David and Oliver and moving so swiftly to the water's edge she seems to float across the rocky ground. I turn away discreetly as she shifts, catching a glimpse of her before she dives deep. She's equally spectacular in seal form, stunning white with the dark star-shaped patch of fur crowning her back.

As the sun sets, David walks to the pyre and mutters an incantation. An icy blue flame flares and the driftwood catches fire, shooting dramatic sparks of teal and orange into the air. The five selkie bodies ignite and the flames consume them, but this magic fire doesn't produce any smoke that might give away our presence.

"Why burn the selkies, and not the seals?" I ask Oliver.

"The seals we'll leave as evidence, in the hope someone from the mortal world finds them," Oliver explains. "But if they examined the selkies too closely... well, it wouldn't be ideal. There are obvious anatomical differences that would be noticeable during a rigorous investigation."

The blue flames mesmerise me and I stand, my thoughts drifting, weak with hunger and misery, and I'm not sure which one has the upper hand. I barely notice Oliver and David, deep in animated conversation, but I catch Oliver leaving, heading to the other side of the island, as David comes towards me. Uh oh. Misery takes the lead.

"Oliver tells me you heard the selkies' distress call." He makes it sound more like an accusation than an observation.

"I think all of Ireland heard those screams." I don't even turn to look at him, keeping my eyes fixed on the fire until he takes a step in front of me. I shiver as his body blocks the heat.

"Not possible. Only selkies can hear each other in pain or fear. That call is mental and emotional—travelling from one selkie mind to another." His face is covered in flecks of blood and dark shadows ring his eyes. He'd look intimidating even without his usual grim expression.

"Then what was it doing in my mind?"

"That's what we want to know." He peers at me quizzically, but all I can do is shrug my shoulders. I don't have the answers, either.

"Is it because I'm bonded to you all?" I wonder.

He shakes his head. "I asked Oliver, and he didn't think so. He's never heard of it happening. If it were part of bonding, then every human bonded to a selkie would hear them in distress. You know Oliver spent years studying the lore. In the tales he recorded, selkies often left and never come back. And the mortals they were bonded to never felt them die or found out what happened to them."

He won't stop staring at me, as if looking at me long enough will reveal the secret. Rather than make me uncomfortable, which is the only effect it's having so far. A change of subject is desperately needed.

"I guess it's a mystery. I have no clue. David?"

"Hmmm?"

"Is your son a selkie? He lost his soul to the sea too, didn't he? If he is one, where is he?"

David breaks off his stare, looking at the ground and muttering something to himself. Probably counting to ten.

"Oliver and Cathal don't know how to keep their mouths shut, do they?" he says finally. He sounds more resigned than angry.

"Don't be mad at them. Be mad at me, for asking such a stupid question."

"It's all right." His eyes seek mine again, but there's less intensity now, mostly sadness. "I guess I should be used to you asking stupid questions by now. My son was alive when he got pulled out of the water. He died in hospital."

"But if you drowned that day, how could you possibly know that?" I'm not trying to be annoying. I'm genuinely puzzled.

"I just know. Now please stop," he says shortly.

"I'm sorry." And I am. He doesn't need to be reminded of death today. It's all around him.

Maybe it's because my brain has tuned itself to their frequency, but I hear a snatch of another selkie distress call building inside my head. It isn't a stabbing scream this time. More like a soft, low moan, an exhausted, defeated sobbing.

"David, I can hear one of them! There must be one still alive."

He stands stock-still, listening with me, before shaking his head.

"That's not anything," he says dismissively.

"But can you not hear it?" I can't stop hearing it, now I've picked it up. It's faint but insistent. "We have to find them! You might be able to save them."

"It's nothing!" His face is stormy, his eyes narrow. I know he doesn't like me, but does he dislike me so much he's willing to ignore a distress call because I'm the one who's hearing it? He's contrary, but he can't be that unreasonable. Can he?

"How can you say that?" I turn to go. "I'm going to tell Oliver—"

"Will you stop! I'm telling you it's nothing!"

He grabs my hand as I move past him and it's like he's lighting one of his magic flames inside me, a spark zipping through my arm when our fingertips touch. His eyes widen, and I know he feels it too.

Before I can even begin to process this potentially disturbing information, he's leaning towards me, the wind whipping his grey hair behind him.

"You think you hear something? How about this?" Gripping my hand tightly, he bumps his lips against mine, almost like he's experimenting to see if it's as crazy an idea as it seems.

The distress call roars louder, filling my mind, unmistakable now and impossible to ignore. I wince with the pain of it and David drops my hand and pulls himself away, taking the sound with him, leaving only the faint echo behind.

"It's me, Marin," he says roughly. "Do you understand now? It's me."

I stare at him. "You?"

"I can't control it. I don't know how to switch it off completely. I've always been this way. Ever since I became a selkie."

"Can Oliver and Cathal hear it?"

"Of course," he says impatiently. "But they're so used to it, they don't even notice it anymore. It's background noise to them. I'm the only one who hears it. And even I mostly tune it out. It's like radio static to me."

He looks crushed, totally defeated and done with me, and I don't blame him. I've managed to make an unbearable day somehow more painful. But when he speaks up again, it isn't to attack me.

"You know I didn't mean it, don't you? When I said you meant nothing?" His words are hushed, almost gentle for someone usually so abrasive. Then, to my surprise, he takes my hand again. "I wanted you so angry with me you'd refuse to be within a hundred miles of where I was. I didn't want you to be in danger." He gives a small, grim smile. "Of course," he adds, "that doesn't mean you're not the most infuriating human I've ever met."

"You haven't met any in a long time." I squeeze his hand and another sudden shock pulses all the way through my veins. "If by infuriating, you mean I'm not compliant and meek, then I think you'll find a lot of us young ones are infuriating these days."

"There's more like you? God help me. In that case, 1955 was a good year to die." I move closer, and he takes my other hand. The flame zips between us like a spark jumping a firebreak. His lips brush mine again, and then he's kissing me, properly this time. His cries of distress pour into my head as the thrill from his touch sweeps through my body. Both surge inside me as his tongue glides in to meet mine. But gradually the sobbing becomes fainter, not as overwhelming. David breaks the spell, pulling back, but only a little.

"It's quieter," he murmurs against my cheek. "You make it quieter."

"David!"

We jump guiltily. Cathal is standing staring at us, his eyes wide, and David shoves me away so hastily I almost fall over. He moves to Cathal who's still rooted to the spot, quaking, his hands shaking by his side. I spot his pelt lying on the ground, discarded on his way to us.

"Cathal! What's wrong? Are you hurt?" David demands frantically, almost shouting.

Cathal shakes his head furiously. The trembling gets worse.

"Talk to me, Cathal. Tell me." David takes him by the shoulder, holding him steady.

"The boat... the ones that did... this..." Cathal's words are so indistinct I have to strain to hear them. "I saw it...caught up with it..." Reaching out, he takes David's arm in both of his.

When he speaks, his voice is shaking as violently as his hands. "It was our old boat. My brother Cian's trawler." Letting go of David, he collapses senseless onto the rocky ground.

THREE DAYS

Oliver moves like he feels every one of his one hundred and thirty years, slumping against me as I sit by the dying fire in the cold light of day. He's come for comfort rather than for the fire, because he doesn't need the warmth of it. Not like I do, weak human that I am. But we're both exhausted after the hours we've spent, taking turns watching over Cathal. After my last time, I took a quick dip in an icy stream running close to the shore to try and freshen up, and I haven't been able to get warm since. I've been huddling under Oliver's pelt, and now I wrap it around both of us. He hardly notices.

"How is he now?"

"He's asleep. David's with him." He drags his hands through his hair, his green eyes shot through with red. "He was so sure we'd go back with him to confront them. He couldn't understand it when we kept telling him no. That boy is more lion than seal."

"It must have been such a shock. Emotional enough to see that boat. And then to realise his brother might have…" I can't finish my train of thought, can't bring myself to follow it to its logical conclusion.

Oliver doesn't reply, staring out over the ocean. I stay quiet, letting his mind rest. He's been through so much, and he looks too fragile for this world. I'm overcome with the need to take care of him. Protect him. Which is ridiculous. He's about a thousand times stronger than I'll ever be.

He speaks again, so suddenly it startles me. "Do you see out there, that choppy body of water?"

Stretching out his long arm, he points beyond us to a channel of white water, leading from the cove below us out into the sea.

"I was returning to Bristol. I had all my research, my notes, everything I owned in the world. They wanted me to wait another day because the conditions were treacherous. But I wouldn't wait. I'd received a letter, telling me my lover was getting married. I'd been away too long. Five years. I was so eager to be home. I needed to stop him, to convince him he was making a mistake. Well, the curragh capsized. I hit my head on it on the way down. So in the end, I was too late anyway. For Christopher. And for the rest of my life." His voice cracks on the last word.

Under his pelt, I slide my arm around his hips, holding him tightly. I grip my other hand in his long fingers where they rest on my knees.

"You've been alone for so long, Oliver. In all those years, did no one call you, before me?"

He leans his head against mine, planting his face in my hair. Inhaling deeply, he sighs. I don't smell like smoky caramel, but maybe I don't smell too awful in comparison. Most probably my scent is like the sea, and to him, that's soothing and familiar. At least I hope so.

"A few times," he says finally. "You're not the first one to cry bitter tears in these waters. There's been so much tragedy here, and pain. Men lost at sea, brothers fighting brothers, poverty and heartache."

"And it didn't work out? They didn't choose..." I'm nervous about asking. Had he answered the call and been refused by someone, before me? I feel bad enough about choosing only one of them. Or none.

"A couple weren't my type, if you understand my meaning," he says, turning pink. "They were lovely women, and I'm ashamed to say I was cold to them. And to the man that called me, too. I told you, Marin, I was dead inside. I wanted to make sure they didn't choose me. It wouldn't have been fair on them. If I agreed to bond with them, it would only be so I could return to the mortal realm and the only person I'd ever love. Although I have to admit, that was nearly enough to tempt me sometimes." His voice breaks, and he clears his throat. "Until it didn't matter anymore, because I knew he would be gone. Nothing but dust."

"You weren't being cold. Not really. They didn't know it, but you were being kind. Like you always are."

My throat closes over as I try to stop the tears from welling. Oliver isn't crying about it, so I have no right to. But somehow he senses my distress. Taking up a corner of his pelt, he uses it to wipe my eyes. It's like him—soft, warm, comforting.

"It heartens me, that you can cry. In my time, it wasn't acceptable behaviour for a man. Like a lot of other things." He gives a rueful smile. "But don't cry for me. It was all so long ago."

His finger follows the curve of my chin, his expression calm and earnest. "Even though you had to witness the terrible things that happened here, I'm glad you're with us. That you called us. You've made me feel some things. Like hope. I think one day, I *will* be able to love someone again. For the first time since I ended up at the bottom of the ocean."

We fold into each other, and I run my hands all over his silky body while he kisses me, no reservations holding him back this time. He takes firm control, setting the pace, teasing my tongue with his, advancing and retreating, always giving me not quite enough of what I want, leaving me aching painfully for more. Shoving me back gently, he lowers his full weight on top of me, and his hard cock presses on mine. Rocking his hips slightly, he rubs himself against me while his tongue explores my ear, his exquisitely scented hair tickling my face.

"Oliver, will you teach me?" I hide my sudden flush of colour in his fair locks. "Will you show me what to do?"

His body stills, and he looks at me. His emerald eyes widen and something unreadable flits across his pale face.

"It's not something you have to learn, Marin," he answers me softly. "It's something your body already knows."

"Please," I almost beg him. Under his weight, I shift my hips, searching for the hard length of his cock so I can press mine even harder against it.

He examines me for a long time, his face serious, and the coil of anxiety winds tightly in my stomach, scared he'll refuse.

"On one condition," he says finally, making my heart trip. "This doesn't mean I'm making a claim on you, do you understand? It won't bond us. It doesn't place any obligation on you."

"I understand," I respond solemnly. "I know you don't feel you can be tied to me."

"What I want doesn't come into it. I'm thinking of what's best for you."

I nod. As he brings his face close to mine, I kiss his pale forehead under his tangled golden hair.

A sudden laugh bubbles out of me. "You're supposed to be the repressed Victorian, and you're the only one of us who knows what he's doing."

He gives a reluctant smile. "I think you should reserve your judgement on that until *after* I've made love to you."

From the way he expertly unbuttons and removes my tattered shirt, it's clear he's being modest. He explores my chest, his fingers pale against my faded winter tan. His mouth chases after his hands, claiming my nipples as his fingers release them. He sucks each of them in turn, teasing them with his tongue while they're still tightening from his touch.

He pulls back, his hands still stroking my chest. "Does everyone have such muscles, these days? Your shoulders rather put me to shame."

"I suppose most swimmers end up looking like this. But there's nothing wrong with your body, Oliver."

As if in response, he pushes his bare chest against mine, and his heart thuds against my skin as his mouth skims mine. Then he's moving down again, his fair head on my stomach as he looks up at me.

I smile in encouragement, and he goes for my trousers, unbuttoning them and sliding them down my legs. He torments me, his mouth circling my stomach and around my thighs as I arch my hips, trying to get him to give some attention to my painfully hard cock. He holds me down.

"All in good time," he breathes. He shifts my legs open and as I reach down to touch the top of his head, I feel the shivery sensation of his tongue flicking my balls, sending a strangled moan tearing from me. He plays with them relentlessly, licking them thoroughly before sucking one of them into his mouth.

"Please." I'm doing a lot of begging. And for such a kind soul, he seems to be enjoying my torment. Finally, when I can barely stand it anymore, he moves to my cock, sliding his tongue up and down it, circling the tip. My mind explodes and my arse clenches as he slides me inside his mouth. Then he's sucking me, his head moving under my hand, alternating his rhythm between fast and frantic and long and slow, using my gasps as his cue when I'm getting too close to the edge.

I know I'm lying on his pelt on solid ground, but the whole world is spinning, a blur, nothing left but me and Oliver and my throbbing cock sliding in and out of the delicious warmth of his mouth. He brings me so close I'm sure I'm going to come squirting onto his tongue before he pulls away and holds me in an expert grip until I'm back under control.

He gives me a questioning look, and I nod at him between shuddering breaths, urging him to keep going. Kneeling up beside me, he takes one of my hands and wraps it around his hard cock. Warm wetness coats my fingers and as my eyes find his, he flushes slightly.

"One of our abilities, as selkies, is that we're... uh... self-lubricating. Do you understand what that means?"

"I think I can feel what that means." I slide my fingers easily down the slick length of him. Releasing his cock, I examine my hand. It shimmers with a silvery residue, sparkling in the light from the fire.

"It looks like it's from some magical creature. Maybe a unicorn."

"It *is* from a magical creature," Oliver corrects me, looking slightly put out. "But one that exists. Unlike unicorns."

Taking him again, I grip him firmly, stroking my hand up and down until his breaths grow ragged. "It seems to be a useful selkie feature."

"Do you mind if I use some of it to... prepare you?" he asks.

I give a small grin. "If it means the difference between pleasure and pain, I'm all in."

"That's only if you want me to—"

"You don't know how much I want you to," I assure him. As if my trembling isn't a dead giveaway.

He pulls away from me, shifting back to my arse. In one deft movement, he lifts my legs and bends my knees, spreading me wide open for him. I watch as he twists his hand around his cock, the silvery liquid collecting in his palm as he pumps on himself. When he's coated his fingers, he moves them to my arse, tracing it gently.

"I can stop anytime, Marin. Just say the word." With that, he slides a finger slowly inside, causing a sudden thrill to spike through me, making me tingle. He works on me patiently, methodically, circling his finger deeper. I feel myself relaxing, opening up, taking him. I give a sudden moan, almost bereft when he slides it out again, but I only feel the loss for a moment before two of his fingers are gliding in. He takes his time, opening me wider, gradually adding another finger. Curling them up inside me, he touches a spot that gives me such a jolt of pure pleasure I squirm on his fingers and my balls contract.

"Oliver," I implore him.

He doesn't answer. Instead, he takes his fingers away, kneeling up to run both hands up and around his cock. Like him, it's long and hard, and it's straining to be inside me. There's a warm buzz from his silvery magic where he's coated my arse generously, leaving me slippery and wet. Rolling the bottom of the pelt, he shoves it under me, lifting me towards him as he swings my legs over his shoulders. He pushes against me, and I try to relax, taking a deep breath. There's only the slightest twinge of pain, gone in a second, before the head of his cock pushes through the tightness and slides inside me.

We groan together and he waits, suspended in time, seeking more reassurance from me. I shift my hips, trying to move him in deeper, and he takes the hint, inching further inside me as the world spins again. I'm breathless, barely able to speak. I nod to him again, and he pushed the full length of his cock in, grasping my cock firmly at the same time.

"Marin, you've gone very quiet. Please tell me I'm not hurting you."

"You're the sweetest man I've ever met Oliver, even if you aren't a man," I gasp out. "Don't worry, I'm fine. More than fine."

"I'll try to hold on for as long as I can," he says regretfully. "But it's been such a long time."

"I don't think I'm that far behind you," I pant.

I give a low moan as he starts to thrust, pulling on my cock in a steady rhythm. As his hand and his hips move harder and faster I know I won't last much longer, with every muscle in my body being pulled unbearably tight and the bottom dropping out of my stomach. In a few more breaths he gives one last deep thrust and it's all over, my come shooting out onto his hand and my stomach. He gives a shout as if the intensity of his orgasm surprises him, and maybe it does, considering how long he's waited for it. He lets my shaking legs drop and there's a warm rush as he slides out of me and collapses on my chest, burrowing his face into my neck.

"I fear that was a very poor first effort. I wasn't expecting it to be over so soon," he whispers into my ear.

"Don't worry, we can go again. Consider it research," I whisper back.

Oliver has taught me quite a bit more about the mysteries of the male orgasm, in the interests of science, by the time we curl up, exhausted, on top of his pelt.

"I think I'll be able to sleep now," he says faintly.

"That's a good idea. You haven't slept in two days." I draw his face down to my muscled chest, and he snuggles in, sighing. A few minutes later his voice is vibrating against my skin.

"I can't sleep. I'm too worried about Cathal."

"But you heard what David said. He'll be okay."

"Not about his health. About his emotional state, when he finds out about this."

"I don't understand how you thought you couldn't feel anything." I rest my hand lightly on his hair. "You care so much. About Cathal. And David."

He lifts his head to look at me, before collapsing back down into the curve of my arm. "Your eyes are such a deep brown," he murmurs. "Like a fathomless pool in a dark forest. I once knew someone with eyes just like yours."

"Christopher?" My fingers slide through his sweaty, tousled locks.

"No." His voice drawls with tiredness. "Someone else."

His breathing deepens. My own eyes droop with weariness. I've slept alone pretty much all my life. The last few nights, I've had warm fur and a warm body to cuddle up to, and I get the feeling it won't be easy to let that go. But I don't have any choice. Because the only thing harder than letting go would be having to choose between them.

~

David comes running over the rise and nearly lands on top of us, jumping away at the last moment. It's dark, and the fire is cold dead ash, the wind chilling my bare skin.

"Oh, excuse me. Sorry. I..." He's momentarily speechless, which must be a new experience for him. He turns his back on us as I gather Oliver's pelt and cover myself hastily. Oliver leaps up, all thoughts of sleep forgotten.

"What is it?"

David twists around, his steely eyes raking over me like knives. I drop my gaze, unable to meet his, my cheeks burning. He speaks again, addressing Oliver. "It's Cathal. He's gone."

TWO DAYS

"He wasn't on Hy-Brasil. I've searched every inch of it." David pulls himself wearily out of the water, clumsy with exhaustion. He's been gone all night, looking for Cathal. "I can't talk to him, either." His face is a tight mask of barely contained emotion. "That means he's not in selkie form."

"You *know* where he's gone. And we must go after him." Oliver's face is calm, but the panic is escalating in his ragged voice.

"Do you not think I tried to find that boat? It was hopeless. It didn't have as much of a head start when Cathal found it, and he knows every wave of this bay. There's no telling how far away it is now. And I won't risk your life, too," David says flatly. "You heard what I said. He's not in selkie form anymore. That means we can't communicate with him, can't trace him. If he's not here or on Hy-Brasil, and he's without his pelt, the most logical conclusion is he's gone against the lore and revealed himself to whoever's on that boat. And you know what that means. He's either dead, or he might as well be."

"Don't say that!" I take his arm, trying to get him to look at me, disturbed by his cold indifference.

"I didn't realise you cared so much about him, Marin. I thought you'd made your choice." His tone couldn't be more vicious, but I let it slide by me without allowing it to sting. If someone's hurting, I'm willing to give them a pass when it comes to acting like a complete jerk. And David, for all his steely exterior, is about as wounded as someone can be and still be alive. He's as mortally wounded as the screaming selkies, only in a different way. It's like he's been slowly dying inside for years. Since the time he physically died. And I won't let it deter me.

"If it's a fishing trawler, it'll probably spend a few more days out at sea, before it heads back to the mainland. All we have to do is follow the usual routes they take until we find it. That's probably what Cathal did. We might still find him in time."

"The bay's a big place. And David and I have only been here every seven years, for a week each time. We don't know the routes," Oliver says.

"All you have to do is follow my directions. I've been swimming in this ocean since I was six years old. I know every current, every rock, every landmark. And I also have some idea of where the fishing trawlers go. It's handy to know if you don't want one to mow you down."

Hope leaps onto Oliver's face at my words, and when I look at David, he's listening to me, grudgingly. I can handle grudgingly. As long as he's listening.

"We don't even know which trawler we're looking for."

"I do," I say firmly. "Cathal told me. It's called Blackbird. You know. After the Beatles song." On second thought, they wouldn't know. "It fishes out of Westhaven, south of Seafort."

"You won't be able to tell us which way to go," David argues. "Not once we're in selkie form."

"Ah, about that." Oliver looks slightly embarrassed. "I meant to tell you. As long as he's touching us, Marin can hear our thoughts after we've shifted."

David can't hold on to his calm coldness any longer. "That's impossible!"

"Well, we can argue about the scientific probability of it another time. Right now, I think there are more important things to be agonising over."

I walk down toward the shore and wade into the water without looking back. I hear two splashes in quick succession and then two bodies are shifting beside me, following me into the waves. I reach for them.

I can't believe you can hear us. Or that I'm trusting you. David's thoughts are as prickly as the rest of him.

And I can't believe I kind of like you, despite everything. Some things can't be explained, I guess. A bit like the existence of selkies.

∼

Nothing.

I hear the despondency in Oliver's thoughts. We've found the trawler and combed the area around it in ever-widening circles, but we still haven't sensed any trace of Cathal.

I have one suggestion left, and it's not going to be a popular one. *You know where he is. The one place we haven't searched. The trawler.*

Not a chance, David growls.

If he's boarded that boat, I can't see a positive outcome being probable, Oliver sighs.

What happens if they see him?

Nothing good, David explains. *Confronting them would be dangerous enough. But it's worse than that. If he's broken the lore and shifted in front of any human who hasn't called him, he's dead anyway. The other selkies will see to that.*

I make my decision. *I'm going after him.*

Not without us, you won't, Oliver insists.

I've got more chance of making it onto the boat without being seen if

I'm alone. You stay here. Don't shift. Someone might be watching. You said it yourself. If they see you, you're dead, one way or the other.

I loosen my grip on their fur and trail my hand down it, taking in the warm silkiness one last time, hoping that isn't what this is. With firm strokes, I swim over to the trawler, careful not to look back. There's a metal ladder leading up to the deck, and quickly I pull myself up, feeling shivery as the wind bites my wet skin, without the warmth of their furry bodies to shield me.

As I swing over the top railing, I hear voices coming from behind a door. Creeping over, I flatten myself against the wall nearest to it, safe in the shadows. My ears prickle as I strain to hear what's happening over the sound of my rushing pulse.

"I'm going to ask you one more time. How did you get on this boat?"

"The same way as you did, sunshine. Up the ladder." My heart leaps at the sound of Cathal's voice. Moments later there's the sharp sting of a slap and I wince for him, but my overriding feeling is giddy relief that he's alive.

"Where did you get this pelt from?" The voice is getting louder and more antagonistic. I can imagine the smile on Cathal's face, inciting his attacker's rage. But he wouldn't be Cathal if he did anything else.

"Could be I slaughtered a seal, same as you did. You managed more than one, though, didn't you? Guess you win. That makes you the fucking hero."

There's another thud and a slight groan and I have barely enough time to push myself against the side of the wall before the door clangs open. The lock turns and several sets of footsteps ring on the deck, getting fainter. I peer out, but there's no one there.

My hands shaking, I flick the lock and swing the door open. And Cathal is there. Smiling, despite his bloody lips, bruised face and the cut over his eye.

"Well, this is a nice surprise." Before I can respond, his face crumples and he bursts into sudden sobs.

My stomach drops. "Cathal! Are you all right? Are you badly hurt?"

"It's not my brother's trawler anymore, Marin. There's none of my family on it."

"Cathal, I'm sorry."

"Don't be sorry." He smiles, even as his tears track through the blood and grime on his face. "I'm glad. If he'd killed those seals, I could never have lived with myself."

I rush forward and hug him fiercely, breathing in his delicious scent. My glance travels downward, and I do a double-take.

"What are you wearing?"

"Waterproofs. They made me put them on. They don't have any problem slaughtering seals, but naked men seem to be an insult to their sensibilities."

"Well, let's go before they come back and you insult those sensibilities some more." I take his hand, trying to pull him towards the door and safety, but he won't move.

"I can't. They have my pelt. I couldn't stop them from taking it. There are six of them and only one of me, amazing as I am. And they have rifles."

"We'll get it back," I reassure him. "We'll get Oliver and David and come back for it. But right now you'll have to swim without it."

He looks at me ruefully. "I think you must have missed the whole bit where I told you I drowned at sea."

Realisation dawns. "You can't swim?"

"'Tis an old fishing superstition," he says matter-of-factly. "If you know how to swim, you're delaying the inevitable. Only takes you longer to die."

For someone like me, who looks at the sea as a refuge rather than an enemy, it's hard to comprehend. But I know from his face he's telling the horrifying truth. "That's totally illogical."

"Hey, don't knock it, it works. At least I didn't spend hours freezing my arse off in the water. Sank like a fecking stone." His hand drops in a rapid movement, miming his trip to the bottom of the ocean.

"You don't think surviving might have been the best outcome?" I say, trying to keep the sarcasm at bay.

"Nah, then I wouldn't have met you."

I slap him on the shoulder. "You're so full of it."

"That's why I sank like a stone," he quips.

I snort with shocked laughter before the door swings open, and we freeze.

I stare at the person standing in front of me. He's wearing Cathal's pelt draped theatrically over his shoulders like a toddler playing dress-up, with two of his misfit crew behind him, clutching their rifles. "Kevin?"

"Marin?" His mouth drops open and stays that way for several seconds before he recovers the gift of speech. "Everyone thinks your dead. They've called off the search and everything. You mean you didn't drown yourself?"

"You think I'd drown myself over you lot? Oh, Kevin, Kevin, Kevin, Kevin."

Cathal winks with the eye closest to me, the one that isn't all cut up. "I'm going to take a wild stab here, but I'm thinking this might be Kevin."

"Well, I like to alternate between that and Gobshite. For variety, you know." I turn back to Kevin. "This trawler used to belong to a Cian Moran. What are you doing with it?"

"How do you know that?" Kevin can't stop looking at me like I'm a ghost. Which I suppose, to him, I am. "He gave up the fishing game and moved away after some family tragedy. My Dad bought this trawler off him years ago. And now he's given it to me. I told you he gave me a boat at the dance. Shows how much you were listening to me," he grumbles. "But what do you care? Where have you been, anyway?" He tips his head towards Cathal. "With this guy?"

"I went for a little island break. Tasket island. I think you know it? And if you don't want anyone to find out what you've been up to there, I'd hand over that pelt now, and let him go."

For a moment, he's quiet, and it looks like he's thinking, as much as Kevin can think about anything. His mouth curls into a familiar sneer.

"I found your friend with a pelt. Who's to know he's not the one killing an innocent protected species? If I say I confronted him and things got nasty, well, it'd be self-defence, wouldn't it? And I wouldn't want anything to happen to you Marin, for you to slip on deck and fall off or something, but here's the thing... people think you're dead."

I roll my eyes, masking my racing thoughts. When I speak again, I keep my face blank and my voice light.

"Kevin, you've been watching too much bad TV. You really need to get out more. That's not how this is going to go. They *thought* I was dead. Past tense. I called my mom from the radio on Cathal's boat. It was moored over the other side of the island. You didn't see it. Too busy slaughtering, I guess. So they're expecting us. And if we don't turn up soon, they'll be coming looking for us. And they'll find you and your little secret. So hand over the pelt, now, if you don't want that to happen. And while you're at it, get Dumb and Dumber to stop poking their guns in our faces."

Kevin frowns, and I can almost hear his brain whirring with the effort of deciding what to do. I stare him down, holding out my hand and hardly daring to breathe, only exhaling when I feel the familiar weight of soft fur. I take it and pass it to Cathal, who accepts it with a grin.

"Come on Cathal, let's go." I make for the door, and Kevin steps in front of me, blocking my exit. He leans into me, grabbing onto my upper arm, his mouth hovering near my ear.

"Kevin. I never knew you cared."

"Tell me the truth," he says in a rasping undertone. "Is my dad your father? Are we brothers?"

I frown. He's more unhinged than I thought. "What are you on about?"

"You heard me," he insists, the words buzzing in my ear.

"Did you think to ask your dad?"

"I did. He said your mom thought she was too good for any of the local lads."

"Well, there's your answer." I wrench myself out of his grip. The two other guys make half-hearted moves toward me, but I stop them with a look. They aren't as eager for a fight when the odds aren't stacked so heavily in their favour, and it isn't defenceless animals they have in their sights.

"He'd never tell me if it were true," Kevin spits. "But you will."

"Why would you even think it's true?" I wonder.

His face hardens, his eyebrows meeting.

"People say things," he blurts out. "Slag me off, tell me I look like you. They always have."

Well, that would explain a lot, even though I can't see the resemblance, myself. And the thought of looking like him isn't something I want to dwell on. But then, he's not all ugly. Only his mind.

"You're not my brother," I say firmly.

"You know that for sure?"

"I do."

I move closer to Kevin, holding his attention with my sincere look, motioning to Cathal to slip out behind us with a nod of my head. As he makes it out onto the deck, I spin around.

"My brother would never be such an arsehole." I jump away from Kevin and over the threshold, slamming the door and spinning the lock shut.

"Come on, Cathal, let's go. There's more of them somewhere." The pounding on the door behind me nearly drowns out my words.

"That was pretty amazing." He gathers me in a huge hug, almost crushing me.

"Kind of like a superhero, wasn't I?"

"Definitely. You're my Superman."

"It's Robin I've always wanted to be. You can be my Batman."

He looks decidedly unimpressed. "I don't want to be Batman. He wears shiny underpants and he can't dance."

I grin. "Don't worry. He's different now. Very dark and sexy."

Cathal rips off the waterproofs, sending them sailing over the side, and we stumble down the ladder. As he holds onto the last rung, about to shift, a face appears over the railing, another one of Kevin's henchmen.

"Hey, you! Stop!"

He isn't brave enough to follow, gathering random objects from the deck and hurling them down the ladder at us instead. A fire extinguisher narrowly misses my head as I grab Cathal's pelt.

"He's watching. You can't shift yet. Oliver told me if you break the lore, the other selkies will punish you. You'll have to get out of sight first."

Cathal's face drops. "I can't, you know that."

"Hold on to me. I've got you. Let go of the ladder!" He hesitates, and his fingers loosen their hold on the rung. I take my chance, wrapping his head in the crook of my elbow and pulling him forcibly off. Swimming hard, I drag him away from the boat. He's so heavy my progress is slow and his pelt drags in the water, acting like an anchor, sabotaging our escape.

"I can't do it, Marin. This is how I died. Sank like a stone, remember? I won't drag you down with me!"

"Stop being so dramatic and let me get you out of here." I refuse to let him sense my slowly rising panic.

"Just let me go!" he shouts.

I kiss him firmly on the top of his head. "Never."

Two seals came shooting like arrows through the water towards us, gliding under us effortlessly, and Cathal and I grab them as they pass. Rapidly they take us out of sight of the trawler, into the wide expanse of the bay, where there's nothing but the crying gulls to witness Cathal shifting back.

When we reach Hy-Brasil, stumbling onto the shore, David shifts back immediately and waits in the shallows, arms folded, anger radiating off him in waves. Oliver follows more slowly, but Cathal stays in his seal form, making his way up the sand by inching along on his belly and collapsing gratefully by my side, nuzzling my foot.

"Don't think you'll avoid my lecture by not shifting back," David huffs.

"You're wasting your time," Oliver says calmly, the voice of reason. "Marin's the only human who can communicate with him in seal form."

"I am?" I ask, surprised.

"It's a bit like a dog trying to understand its owner, when one of us is in selkie form, and the other is human," Oliver explains. "We get the general gist from the tone and facial expressions, but that's about it."

We're certainly getting the general gist from David now, which makes Cathal even less likely to return to his human form.

"You shift back, now. Do you hear me, young man?" David bends down and Cathal looks at him with his liquid golden eyes and sweet seal face, the picture of innocence.

David throws up his hands. "This isn't over. You can't avoid me forever, and when you shift back, so help me, I'll—"

"Maybe it's time you backed off," I interrupt him. "Controlling everyone you love won't change what happened to your son."

His eyes glint coldly at me, but I can take it. At least I've distracted him from Cathal. For the moment.

"You have no idea what you're talking about," he mutters.

"No, I don't. But I've seen enough. And I've never seen a pair more loyal to anyone the way Cathal and Oliver are to you. And still, you give them a hard time. Constantly."

Before he can respond, Oliver steps in.

"David, Cathal's injured. Let him rest. We can discuss this later." He puts a conciliatory hand on David's shoulder and leads him away. He risks giving me a wink as they disappear down the beach.

Is he gone? Cathal asks.

Yes, he is, you awful man, I reply.

I prefer mammal. It covers both sides of me.

Pinniped, if you want to be specific, I correct him. *It means wing-footed.*

You know your seals.

Some of them.

I avert my eyes for a few seconds so Cathal can take his human form. He sprawls out beside me, giving me a wink.

"I'm sorry to put you in danger. I'm such an eejit. I don't deserve saving, but thank you anyway."

"Are you serious? I haven't had that much fun in a long time." I smile with satisfaction, remembering the look on Kevin's face as I slammed the door on him.

"I hate to desert you so soon after your rescue, but I need a swim in the stream." The sweaty fear that engulfed me when I wasn't sure if Cathal was alive is clinging to me, despite our trip back through the water.

"I'll join you. I want to wash the smell of that trawler, and Kevin, out of my hair. Now that's someone who does smell of fish."

Remembering what happened to get us onto that trawler, I'm suddenly sober, my face tight.

"I'll make sure he doesn't get away with what he did, Cathal," I promise. "When I get home."

"You might not have to do it alone," he says softly, making my heart hurt.

We splash around for a while, no self-consciousness between us, enjoying the moment of being together. When we're done, Cathal stretches his pelt out on the bank near the stream and lies behind me, both of us naked. I don't protest very much. It gives me a warm feeling, to have him so tightly against me, our fingers intertwined as he holds both my hands. After a while, he stirs, restless.

"Marin, when you said you'd never let me go, did you mean it? Because you know tomorrow is the day this place disappears."

Light kisses rain down on the back of my neck and along one shoulder. I melt under his bombardment of affection.

"Marin?" he asks again. "Because, I've been thinking about it, and maybe you shouldn't choose me."

I feel a sudden chill under the warm sunshine. "You don't want me to?"

"I didn't say that. But I think Oliver or David need to be bonded more than I do. It's not a bad life, here. I kind of like it. I don't feel like I need to be free. It'd almost be wasted on me. They'd get a lot more out of it. In some ways, I feel like I got my freedom already, when I became a selkie."

I turn around to face him, my heart heavy. "Let's not waste time talking about it. Let's just make the most of every last second."

He starts singing It's Now or Never at the top of his voice, and I decide this isn't the time to tell him Elvis was another casualty of the rock and roll lifestyle.

I take his shoulders and roll him on top of me until his beaming face is inches from mine. He lands more kisses on my neck and runs his tongue slowly to the base of my throat. He slides down further, taking my nipple into his mouth and biting hard.

"Mmm, still salty." Moving back up, he grazed my lips with his.

"So are you. Salty and sweet. And smoky. And wild."

He starts humming Wild Thing by the Troggs.

"Did I mention a dinosaur?"

"Hey, less of the insults about my age."

"I was more referring to your taste in music."

"Careful, buachaill. Those songs are timeless classics. Like me."

Holding on to me tightly, he rolls, flipping us over expertly, so I'm lying on top.

"Nice trick."

"Very small sleeping bunks in a trawler." He winks. "You pick up some things."

Holding on to my waist, he sits me up, swinging my legs on either side of him so I'm on my knees, straddling his hips, his firm cock underneath me. He grinds it against my arse while my toes curl and my cock twitches in response. A moan escapes me.

"Seems you appreciate a timeless classic." He grins.

"I'm not too heavy for you, am I?"

He shakes his head, and I bend forward until his face is close to mine. He showers me enthusiastically in wet kisses like an excited puppy. I take a handful of his hair, trying to slow him down.

"Your lip is all bashed up. You'll hurt it more," I protest.

"I can't feel anything except where it matters."

I answer him with kisses, long and deep. He lifts his hips, grinding himself into me again while my cock, trapped between us, rubs his firm stomach. Making a thousand butterflies beat their wings against my skin.

"You're very flexible," he remarks. "Bendy."

"Double-jointed," I explain. "Comes in handy sometimes. Especially if you're a swimmer." I sit up again, easing myself down his body. Settling into position, I bend down and take his firm cock into my mouth.

He jumps, almost pulling away, but stops himself in time.

"Jaysus," he mutters breathlessly. "I wasn't expecting that. No," he adds hastily, as I hesitate. "Don't stop."

A thrill of excitement spins through me as I suck on him, and his appreciative moans only intensify the feeling. I mightn't have Oliver's skill, not yet, but it doesn't seem to matter to either of us. Threading his fingers in my curly hair, Cathal thrusts his hips, pushing his cock deeper into my mouth. It gags me, making me jerk my head back and his face drop.

"Sorry, Marin. I got carried away. I'm hopeless—" I put a finger to my lips, silencing him with a look, and slide his throbbing hardness back onto my tongue. More controlled now, he takes the time to experiment until he's able to fuck my mouth with exactly the right technique to make my balls buzz and my legs go weak. His exotic scent explodes in my nostrils as the taste of sweet saltiness fills my mouth. Of course. He has the same silvery magic as Oliver. His cock slides even more easily in and out, and I try not to get carried away with the thought of it sliding into my arse.

As if reading my mind, Cathal gazes at me intently, his golden eyes even brighter than usual, watching me on my knees in front of him, my arse up in the air.

"I wish I could take you, exactly like that," he murmurs.

His words made me quiver, and I release his cock.

"Why can't you?" My voice shakes.

"Come on, you know I'm clueless. I wouldn't know where to start."

"Let's start at the very beginning, a very good place to start," I sing tunelessly.

"The Sound of Music. I know that film," he answers with a flashing grin.

"At least someone does. Come on, what's the worse that can happen?"

"I make a total mess of it, do everything wrong and you never want to see me ever again."

"Did that happen to you a lot?" I tease him.

I stay where I am, resting my elbows on his pelt, and eventually, he slides out from underneath me. My heart twists when I sense him move in behind me.

"Holy fuck Marin, you look so good," he says breathlessly. "Those legs. Those shoulders. That tight arse."

"Let's concentrate on the arse for now," I coach him. "You do know you're self-lubricating, right?"

"Of *course* I do. I'm not that innocent. I had to do something for entertainment around here. It's a habit I picked up on those long fishing trips."

"Too much information," I tell him, trying not to laugh. "Please be serious, or I'll lose my erection."

"That I can do something about." One of his large hands wraps around my cock, while the other one cupped my balls. He pumps me energetically until I start to squirm.

"You have to stop, I'm going to come."

"Penis locked and loaded. Disaster averted. See, all that practice on myself came in handy."

I stifle another laugh, anxious not to undo all his hard work. "For feck's sake, just fuck me, you eejit, before I change my mind."

"I'm getting a distinct feeling of déjà vu."

His hand releases me and his cock rubs against me again, hard and insistent, and all of a sudden laughing is the furthest thing from my mind.

"You can use some of your silvery stuff, to make it easier. Put it on your fingers."

"I'd prefer to get you ready this way," he murmurs, and my stomach flips as his cock disappears and instead his hot wet tongue circles my arse.

"Yeah, that works," I stammer.

He licks and sucks, taking his time, teasing my arse into opening up for his tongue while I try not to pass out from the sensation. He trails down my crack, sweeping lower and licking the tender skin there before he subjects my arse to more unrelenting exquisite torture. When he eventually slides one finger and then two inside me, I barely feel them.

My ears ring as Cathal rubs his cock all over my arse and in between my cheeks, spreading his silvery magic, leaving me groaning.

"Here goes nothing," he says nervously.

"It doesn't feel like nothing," I reply.

The head of his cock pushes against me and grabbing my hips, he thrusts inside, faster and less cautiously than Oliver. I guess it's true he's more impulsive. But I'm beyond caring, desperate for him.

"Fuck me," he gasps.

"That's my line."

One of his hands moves from my hip to take my cock. I thrust into his hand as he fucks me harder. "I don't think I'm going to last long, Marin," he confesses.

"I'm starting to think premature ejaculation is a selkie thing."

"I think you'll find it's more of a haven't had sex in forever, thing," he breathes. "And in my case, never with a fella."

But in the end, he holds on, finding his rhythm, and every part of me tingles and burns as he pushes me closer and closer to the edge. As it turns out, I get there before him, throbbing and spasming in his hand, and he comes immediately after me, shuddering and groaning. Slowly he catches his breath.

"Like riding a bike," he mutters, and I know by his voice that he's grinning.

ONE DAY

The smell of baked fish greets me the next morning, the light bright behind my eyelids. In many ways being kidnapped and taken to a mythical island has been the sun holiday most people would kill for. Minus the seal massacres, bad guys on boats, and a bizarre supernatural version of blind dating.

The first thing I notice is Cathal is gone. But so is his pelt, so he's probably in the water somewhere. Crouched beside the fire, tending to the fish, is David. His face is serious, but he seems calmer, and I hope Cathal has escaped the worst of his wrath. As I look at him, he turns to me and smiles, a warm, genuine smile, deepening all the fine lines that make his grey eyes even more compelling.

"Morning." He hands me a large leaf with berries, nuts and fish artfully arranged on it.

"Good morning. Thanks. Where's Cathal and Oliver?"

"Hunting for their breakfast. They'll be back in a while." He claps his hands together. "So, last day?"

"I suppose it is."

We eat and the silence stretches out. Hmmm. This isn't awkward at all.

I can see he's hesitating, pulling on his ear while he considers what to say next. He has very sexy ears, if that's a thing. They're neat and close to his head, but not too small. In fact, he's a bit like that all over. He doesn't have as much body hair as Cathal on his chest and stomach, but he isn't silky smooth like Oliver, either. And he isn't as lean as Oliver or as muscular as Cathal, but he definitely has a six-pack. He's one of those just-right sort of men, with no extremes, everything in the middle. He coughs, and I drag my eyes up to his face. He's caught me checking him out, but I don't care.

"Marin?"

"Yeah?"

"Have you forgiven me for plucking you from the sea? Because I wouldn't like to think of you out there somewhere, hating me."

"I don't hate you. I never did."

He gives me a doubtful look.

"I might have resented you a small bit, in the beginning."

"That's better." He chews on his lip anxiously before speaking again. "I was hoping to spend a little time with you today. If you don't mind."

Surprisingly, I don't mind. My original plan was to cram in as much time with Cathal and Oliver as I could, while I could, but getting to know more about David is an intriguing prospect. If I hadn't been so annoyed with him from the start, I might have realised earlier how flustered I get when he's around, and how my insides twist when I catch him looking at me. And this new, friendly David only intensifies that feeling.

He holds out his hand and slowly opens it, presenting me with a long strip of cloth.

"What's this?"

"Here. Put on this blindfold."

"David, you kinky thing. I had no idea."

There's a glimpse of the old exasperated David as he sighs.

"So you can't see where we're headed. I want it to be a surprise."

"Sorry. Only messing with you. Hand it over, so."

He smiles in response, and it's a no-holds-barred stomach flipper, designed for maximum impact. If I were to choose one of them based objectively on looks, David is the most attractive. But he's also the most closed off, the hardest one to get to know. I wonder if it's too late to find out who he really is before I have to leave. I like this David, the one who isn't trying to keep his emotions chained up in the basement.

A few minutes later and we're in the water, David's soft silver fur familiar by now to my hands. We exchange a few silent thoughts, checking in on each other, and then I relax and enjoy the moment, revelling in the freedom of gliding through the waves. The weather changes the farther we go, the water gradually becoming colder, icy raindrops stinging my head. Once or twice a stray wave buffets me before David pulls me towards calmer waters.

Can I look now?

Soon.

More time passes before something ripples in my hands and David is shifting back to human form, right there in the deep water. I've seen him tackle the water in his mortal form. Unlike Cathal and Oliver, he's a strong swimmer. Observing him, I realised that only bad luck or freak currents could have made him drown. Now his strong arms grasp me tightly, wrapping himself around me as we tread water. He rips off the blindfold and my breath stutters when I take in our surroundings. He lifts his heavy pelt effortlessly out of the water and slings it around both of us.

We're about a mile from the shore of the bay. In the distance, I can see the stretch of rocks and sand where I first waded into the water.

"This is where you rescued me."

"You mean kidnapped you."

I laugh and then he joins in, properly. It transforms his face, his eyes flashing like quicksilver before he turns serious again.

"I'm sorry for kidnapping you. I've brought you home, Marin."

I stare at him, but he refuses to look at me, fixing his eyes on the shoreline, towards the rocks and hills. But my face is right up against his, close enough to see the small tear working its way down his cheek, almost lost in the briny droplets covering his face.

I shake my head. "What are you saying? I can't go back home yet. I haven't decided anything."

"You don't have to choose any of us. Or them. I know I'm not really in the running." He turns back, giving me a small, sad smile. "What I mean is, you deserve more than to be tied to one of us. Whoever you choose, they'll never be fully there for you. They'll always be longing for the open sea and the selkie life, as well as wanting you."

Twisting, I wrench myself away from him, darting out from under his pelt. "I could handle that. I wouldn't want anyone's life to revolve around me anyway. I'll be busy chasing my own dreams." I examine him earnestly. "Do you not want me to break the curse for at least one of you, to be able to come and go as you please, not be a hostage in the Otherworld? And even if I don't choose any of you— how do you think Oliver and Cathal will feel if I leave without saying goodbye?"

"They'll get over it. They have me." Frustration darkens his face. "Why do you always have to be so stubborn? I'm trying to make this easy for you."

"That's very noble of you, David," I say calmly. "And it's also bullshit. Now, tell me the real reason you brought me back. Because I know you have one."

"It's not what you're thinking," he says quickly. "You think I don't want you around. But that's not true."

I must admit that was my first thought. He never wanted me there in the first place. It wouldn't be much of a stretch to believe he can't wait for me to go so it can be just the three of them again. But gazing at him, I see straight through his steel, all the way to his vulnerable heart. Maybe I have superpowers after all. And as always, in the back of my mind, there's the faint echo of his anguish.

I take his arm. "Then tell me! Why?"

He's trembling, changing, shifting again, back to his seal form. For a second I'm sure he's abandoning me, leaving me with nothing but my old life. Well, if that's what he wants, he'll have a fight on his hands. I hold onto his fur like letting go would mean drowning too.

But now he's sending me thoughts. Or not thoughts, exactly. Memories. I see this exact place in my mind, but it looks slightly different. There's a boy with auburn hair swimming beside me. Not swimming. He's struggling, going under. We're both trapped in a relentless current, being pulled out to sea.

I can tell he's exhausted, unable to take much more. He goes under again, slipping from my clumsy tired arms. I try to dive in after him, but I can't see him in the water—it's too murky. I search frantically and finally snatch a lock of his hair, enough to pull him up. I drag him with desperate newfound strength, stumbling with him onto the rocky shore. Waiting arms take him from me, trying to soothe me, wrapping something warm around me. I try to fight them as his limp form is carried away from me, and then it goes black.

David shifts back, searching my confused face anxiously.

"You got him to shore. You were alive. I don't understand—"

"I couldn't live without him. I figured we'd be reunited in death. Or so I thought. So I came back here and let the sea take me." He gives me a rueful look.

The truth hits me like a truck. "That's what you thought I was doing."

"Most people don't wade into the ocean with their clothes on, sobbing their hearts out. Not if they're planning on coming back."

"I wasn't *sobbing*," I correct him, as stubborn as always. I squeeze his arm tighter. "You didn't want me to do what you did. That's why you went for me like that. And why you were sort of angry with me afterwards."

He doesn't deny it. "Please, Marin," he implores me. "Swim back home. Don't choose at all. If you choose between them, one of them will have to break the other's heart. It'll tear us apart. And I won't survive it—losing them. Losing my family. Not a second time."

As I gaze at his stricken face, Réalta Dubh's words ring clear in my mind. *Sometimes, Marin, the best choice is not to make one.* All of a sudden, I understand what she was trying to tell me. And I know what to do.

I move my face closer, the roar of his pain swamping my mind for an instant as my lips gently brushed his.

"I promise you, David. You have my word. I'll never come between any of you, or make you live without each other. But let me go back. I need to talk to them, one last time."

He nods, and when our lips touch again, the heat between us ignites, like magical fae fire, white-hot, sparks flying. It burns through his sorrow, devouring it, and once again his cry of distress fades to a faint whisper in my mind.

David breaks away. "That felt dangerous," he says darkly.

"You really need to learn to lighten up."

"I think we just did."

I look at him closely. "David, did you make *a joke*?"

We kiss each other again, sweeter and slower, the energy zipping around us like sparklers on a birthday cake. After a while, I sigh and reluctantly pulled away.

"Come on. It's time."

David's fingers dig into my arm. "We don't have to tell them about this. They don't need to know. It's bad enough I have to see you break their hearts, without them knowing you're bruising mine too."

I stare at him. "I am?"

He doesn't answer, but he doesn't need to. A part of me has always known it, from the first time I heard his pain and chased it away with a kiss.

I give him a quick slap on the arse. "Hurry up and shift." To my amazement, Mr Silver Fox control freak obeys. We race back with exhilarating speed, and it isn't long before we coast into the warm waters of Hy-Brasil.

Cathal and Oliver are standing on the shore, looking in our direction. Without even waiting for David to shift back, I wade towards them, splashing water everywhere with my frantic leaps. Finally, I'm on the sand and I fling one arm around each of them, holding them in a fierce grip, Cathal's warm muscles and Oliver's soft lean back sending joy spiking through me.

"I'm not choosing one of you," I announce hoarsely.

Cathal clears his throat. His firm hand clasps one of my curly locks, wrapping it around his finger. "That's okay, Marin," he says softly into my ear. "We gave it our best shot."

"You all love each other so much, I couldn't break you apart," I choke out. "Even if I could choose between you. Which I can't."

"Don't upset yourself," Oliver soothes me. "We understand. We'll take you home."

"Shut up and let me finish," I order shakily. "What if I chose all of you? Do you think you'd be okay with that? I mean, is it even possible?"

They stand silent and still, their arms around me.

"I know it's acceptable under the ancient Brehon laws of Ireland, the ones the immortals still follow. David?" Oliver turns to where David is standing knee-deep in water, his face unreadable.

"There's nothing to say you can't," he replies carefully. "But I've never heard of selkies sharing a mate."

"First time for everything," Cathal says with a grin.

"It'd be an interesting case study," Oliver adds with a shy smile.

"Does that mean?" I look from one to the other, my heartbeat marking the seconds, counting down my fate.

Then Oliver is taking me by my broad shoulders and lifting me off the ground, and Cathal's laugh, like great bells ringing, echoes along the beach. I sense their happiness rising to match my own. But it doesn't feel right. Not yet. I wriggle out of their tight hug and call to David, standing in the same spot, watching warily.

"I want all of you. Do you not get it, David? All. Of. You." His face turns stormy and for a second I think he's going to argue, until he cracks and breaks, running to wrap us in his protective embrace.

DAVIS LAVENDER

Now, I can feel it. The bond tightening around us, never to be undone.

∼

"Three pelts are definitely better than one." I stretch out, David on one side of me, Oliver on the other.

"Speak for yourself. My arse is hanging off the edge," Cathal complains over Oliver's shoulder.

"Here," Oliver says impatiently. Turning to face Cathal, he grabs him by the shoulders and rolls them both over in one graceful movement, so he's on the outside and Cathal is next to me.

"So, shagging in narrow bunks was a Victorian thing too?" Cathal asks.

Oliver frowns. "As usual, I have no idea what you're talking about. Is that better?"

"Considerably," Cathal says, leaning in to kiss me. I'm not sure about kissing him back at first, not with David and Oliver there. Until David trails his lips along my neck, running his hand down my side and resting it on my thigh. If he doesn't feel self-conscious in front of the others, I probably shouldn't either.

Giving in, I respond to Cathal eagerly, and he unbuttons my shirt by touch as I fall into his sweet kisses. David's deft fingers make short work of my trousers, and he pulls them down off me. Pushing into Cathal, I feel his strong muscles sending heat against my firm body, his cock hardening next to mine.

My breath catches as David moves his body closer, his cock hot and stiff next to my arse. It feels like the rest of him. Just right.

While he's still kissing me, Cathal takes my cock and gathers it up with his, wrapping his hand firmly around them. He pulls on us both, my hardness against his as he slides his hand up and down with the help of the shimmery silver magic, while my hips jerk and my skin shivers. Eventually, he releases me, moving back so he can look at me.

86

"I'd like to be the one to have someone inside me, this time," he says softly. "What do you think, Marin?"

Confusion clouds my mind, and I'm torn. I don't want to disappoint him. But I don't feel ready to do what he's asking, and I'm not sure it will ever really be for me, either. Then I notice Oliver's hand, pale against Cathal's hip, and all of a sudden, everything makes sense.

"If that's what you want..." I reach up to push one of his spiky strands off his face. "You couldn't do better than Oliver."

"Oliver?" Cathal doesn't even sound that surprised, and he doesn't seem upset. Or unsettled by the idea. Almost as if he's realised it too. Oliver's face appears above Cathal, looking wary, but far from stunned.

"You know what's going on here, don't you?" I ask him.

"Tell us." David's voice is husky in my ear.

"Before you bonded to me. Maybe even a long time before." I look into Cathal's golden eyes. "You bonded to each other, without even realising it. That's why you all answered my call."

"That is one conclusion," Oliver says cautiously.

"The only one that makes sense. To explain how you feel about each other, and me."

"Sounds good to me," Cathal declares. "I'm open to the possibility. And so is my arse."

"Must you be so crude?" Oliver sighs.

"C'mon. You love it. You love me. Isn't that what Marin's saying?"

Oliver doesn't answer, just plants his lips on Cathal and gives him a heartfelt kiss that makes my insides swoop like I'm on a rollercoaster. He grabs Cathal's hips from behind and pulls them towards him, cradling him in his lap. Following his lead, David stirs into action, his hands reaching down to spread my cheeks. He growls deep in his throat as he slides his throbbing length between them. I lean back into him, twisting my face until his tongue plunges into my mouth. I barely notice the low throb of his distress call this time, nearly drowned out as it is by the other sounds he's making. I only break away from him to kiss Cathal again.

Cathal's strong hand closes over my cock, and I take his in mine. We pump each other in rhythm as David glides his cock up and down my arse and Oliver holds Cathal firmly from behind. From the blissful look on Cathal's face, I can guess what Oliver is doing with his skilful fingers.

"You feel ready, physically," he says after a while. "Let me know when you're ready otherwise."

"I might never be ready, so you may as well go for it," Cathal answers cheerily. He shudders against me when Oliver slides inside him, and he leans in and kisses me hard, biting down on my lip before pulling away.

"Fuck me," he mutters.

"Got it right this time," I grin. A moan wipes the smile from my face as the head of David's cock pushes against the opening of my arse.

"So, *boy*, do you want me?" he teases me in a low voice, making me flare up, but this time not in anger. "I think you've always wanted me. You can't wait to have my cock inside that sweet tight arse of yours."

"This is the one time I don't mind you being bossy," I gasp.

"That's big talk, David. Do you even know what to do?" Cathal pants out, managing a smirk.

"Listen to him. One shag and he's an expert," David says. "I'm relying on my instincts. It's not exactly a fucking science. Sorry, Oliver," he adds.

"It *is* a science. Biology," Oliver objects between jagged breaths.

I've had enough of the theory, pushing back against David to signal my raw need. He's rubbed me all over with so much of his magic, I'm feeling confident enough to take him. Answering his question, I let him ease himself inside my arse, inch by delicious inch. He murmurs my name like a chant as he fucks me and I watch Cathal's eyes close in his sweaty face as Oliver rocks behind him, the thrill of it making my heart race. I pull on Cathal's cock again, matching Oliver's thrusts. Cathal is still clutching mine, but he's oblivious now to anything but Oliver inside him. I know what that's like, and I don't blame him for a second. Suddenly David closes his hand over Cathal's, guiding it up and down my cock, and I have to close my eyes too, so I can concentrate on not coming too soon.

"David," I say softly. His pain is barely a whisper in my head and getting fainter all the time.

"Marin!" Shouting my name, he clutches at my cock convulsively as with long powerful thrusts he comes throbbing inside me. He stays there resting for a few seconds, sighing against my back. Then with trembling fingers, he moves Cathal's hand harder and faster until a wave roars in my ears and I'm coming too. It's only a few heartbeats before I hear Oliver's muffled cry and feel Cathal's come hot and sticky on my hand.

Rolling onto my back, I lie between them, hearing their jerky breathing as I try to get my ragged pulse under control. As the pounding in my ears recedes, I cock my head. "Listen."

David stirs beside me.

"I can't hear anything," he grumbles.

"Exactly." I turn to face him, just in time to see the understanding dawn in his quicksilver eyes.

～

"Will it work?" I ask Oliver.

"There's only one way to be sure. We must test our hypothesis."

"Whatever he said. Let's go." Cathal shuffles impatiently.

"The sun is setting. We haven't got much time." David lifts his arms and starts herding us towards the ocean.

We keep our thoughts and our fears to ourselves on our trip back to the bay. Oliver had already explained to us that whoever I bonded to could remain with me, in my world, after Hy-Brasil disappeared.

But he didn't know what would happen if I tried to bond with three of them. Even if they were bonded to each other.

As we reach the shore, the waves are like liquid gold, the sky a deep pink, Hy-Brasil a small triangle, barely discernible on the very edge of the horizon. My selkies shift and we stand, my arms wound tightly around Cathal and Oliver on each side of me, as David holds me closely from behind.

"In case this isn't successful, I want to make you aware that I..." Oliver's gentle voice stumbles, then stops.

"What the poor, posh lad is trying to say, Marin is that I, I mean we, that is..." Cathal trips over his words.

"You'll always be ours. Our bonded mate. No matter what." David was the last one to bond himself to me, but he's the first to say it, his chin resting in my hair, his body firm against mine.

"Same." I say it softly, overcome with sudden shyness.

The sun slowly disappears over the edge of the world. Hy-Brasil shimmers like a heatwave, rippling as we watch.

"The suspense is killing me," Cathal groans, holding my hand so tightly he cuts off the circulation to my fingers. Oliver and David say nothing, quiet except for their laboured breathing. I don't seem to be able to breathe at all.

The last of the light leaks away, the darkness chasing it across the water. I check the horizon again and again, just to make sure.

"Oliver?"

"It appears to have gone."

"And we're still here," Cathal says, sounding uncertain.

"Stating the obvious," David teases him, his voice cracking with relief. He envelopes me in a hug so tight my bones almost pop, while Cathal bounces up and down like a lunatic. Taking Oliver's hands, he swings them both around and around on the beach, whooping and hollering.

"Really, Cathal, you're making a total spectacle of yourself." Oliver gives a shy grimace, but I can tell he's almost enjoying it.

"Marin." A very familiar voice cut across our celebrations, and I turn to see someone standing there, watching us. Small and thin with a strong, determined face and a warm smile. My mother. The three lads hastily snatch up their pelts while I run to her and hug her tightly.

"Mom!"

She feels horribly frail, especially after all the selkie muscle I've become accustomed to. But there's a solidness to her too, in her straight back and wiry arms. She takes them now and gently pushes me away, holding me at arm's length, my hands in hers. She takes in the tattered, stained remnants of my suit.

"I won't ask you how the dance went. Must have been quite a night. Your good suit, it's slightly... ruined, isn't it?"

"A small bit."

"They told me you drowned." Her chin trembles. "They found your jacket. But I couldn't bring myself to believe it. Not my boy, who always loved the sea so much. You'd never want it for a grave. And when we were searching, I saw Hy-Brasil, on the horizon. I had some hope to cling to, then. I knew that if you were alive, if you were coming back to me at all, I only had to wait. Seven days." She looks over my shoulder.

"Aren't you going to introduce me to your young men?"

"I don't think young is the most appropriate description." I lead her over to them, and she seems unperturbed by the three semi-naked men standing in front of her. She's obviously much better at handling this type of situation. She shakes their hands one by one, repeating their names back to herself in that calm, pleasant way she has with people. Then, with Oliver's hand in hers, she speaks again.

"Tell me, Oliver, do you know a selkie named Miah?"

Oliver's eyes widen and he takes a sharp breath. "Did *you* know him?"

"How is he?" she asks.

His face falls. "He died. Some time ago."

"How long?"

"Let me see." He frowns thoughtfully, considering. "Seventeen years."

"Thank you." She pats Oliver's hand gently. "He told me about you, you know. All of you."

She lets him go and takes my hand in hers. "Open it."

I obey and she takes something out of her pocket and places it on my palm. I recognise it instantly. A mermaid's tear, shining in my hand like the sunlit sea. She closes my fingers over it.

"Your father gave that to me, right here on this beach. I said no to him. Because I was afraid of what it would do to him if he stayed. The way he talked about his pod, I knew how much they depended on him, and I didn't want to be the one to make him leave. But I asked him to come back in seven years, in case I changed my mind. You and I came here every one of those seven days. I couldn't wait for him to find out about you. You played in the water, and I waited. But he never came back, no matter how many tears I cried into the sea."

"Well, fuck me," Cathal exclaims.

David frowns at him, before lifting his eyebrows at Oliver. "That explains a lot."

"I told you the most probable explanation was that he had some sort of selkie lineage." Oliver sounds delighted with himself. Once a scientist, always one. "Miah's son," he says, quieter this time, and his green eyes glow as he looks at me.

I gather my father's bonded mate into another tight hug. "I'm so sorry, Mom."

She pats my back. "Don't be, sweet boy. Deep down, I always knew the answer. He would have come back to me if he could."

She steps back again and looks over at my selkies, considering them thoughtfully. They stand there, almost bashful, holding tightly onto their pelts.

"I'm so glad you found them," she says. "But... all three of them?"

I smile sheepishly. "It's one of those package deals. They only came as a set."

EPILOGUE

"Are you sure you can't shift?" Cathal asks.

"I told you. I've tried so many times in the last couple of days. I guess I didn't inherit that bit."

"He needs to lose his soul to take selkie form, you simpleton," Oliver says with a sigh.

"And that could be difficult, considering he doesn't have one." David gives me a knowing smile, daring me to rise to the bait.

"They must have made an exception for you," I throw back at him.

"He's got you there, David." Cathal's booming laugh echoes along the street, but nobody turns to look. Nothing about us would draw anybody's attention. We could be any group of friends, sitting outside the seaside cafe, enjoying the rare winter sunshine. The guys are getting used to wearing human clothes again, at least in public. And when my mom's around.

"Who's that?" Oliver sounds curious, and I turn to see a group of men approaching us. Make that, boys. Kevin and two of his friends are headed in our direction.

"Not this eejit again," Cathal mutters.

Kevin stops in front of us, not making any attempt to hide his stares, taking a good look at my companions.

"Well, Marin, I see you're still alive."

"I see you're not in prison," I say shortly. "Yet."

He looks over at Cathal. "So, how's your boyfriend?" His tone is venomous.

I let it pass. He has to be him for the rest of his life. That's punishment enough.

I grasp Cathal's hand. Taking his cue, Oliver reaches across the table and grabs my other one. David drapes an arm over my shoulder.

"They're great, Kev, thanks for asking," I respond breezily. He turns pale, his mouth falling open. We watch him storm off down the street, twitching with indignation, his friends trailing after him.

"I'm not sure we can stay here much longer. Or my mom, either. This village isn't quite big enough. And I don't think it's ready for us yet."

"I'm not sure it'll ever be ready for me." Cathal's laugh rings out again.

"Not while you keep making a spectacle of yourself," Oliver chides him gently. He turns to me. "We should bring your mother to see your grandmother, anyway. Miah's mother. It's about time they met."

"I have a grandmother?"

"Of course you do. Ré. Réalta Dubh. Dark Star."

"The leader of the selkies is my *grandmother*?"

"Did I not mention that?" Oliver asks innocently.

David hugs me closer. "We can leave whenever you like. We're free to go anywhere you want to. And not only in this realm."

His sparkling eyes, full of warmth, hold mine as I grin at him. The magic finally came through for this wary, tongue-tied loner of a kid. I'm going somewhere else. Anywhere else. And I'm not going alone.

THE END...

Thanks for reading *Selkie Sea*!

If you're ready for some more fantasy, this time a lot longer and a little lighter, you might like to try my warm, fuzzy MM fantasy romance *Dragon Falls (How to Tame a Husband)*.

You can also join my newsletter at davislavender.com or my Facebook group Davis Lavender - Readers' Lounge to get access to giveaways, ARC opportunities and bonus stories every month.

BOOKS BY DAVIS LAVENDER

Selkie Sea

(standalone novella)

The Dragon Falls Series

Dragon Falls (How To Tame a Husband)

Dragon Lands (How to Tame an Enemy)

(coming 2023)

Dragon Peaks (Hot To Tame a Wild Boy)

(coming 2024)

About Davis Lavender

I've written everything from angsty but sweet MMMM fantasy to fun, cozy MM fantasy. But one thing is certain — my heroes (and anti-heroes) will always get their happily ever after.

Living in a small seaside village in Ireland, I haven't given up hope of running into a selkie (dragons may prove to be more elusive).

In between writing, I wrangle cats, watch Asian dramas and ugly cry over the fates of fictional characters.

Please feel free to stalk me on Facebook and join my group, Davis Lavender - Readers' Lounge, for exclusive access to giveaways and bonus content, or sign up for my newsletter at davislavender.com.

You can also email me at davis@davislavender.com.

Printed in Dunstable, United Kingdom

76363540R00066